# Heart of Africa

## Dedication

To Jack, who loves all the wild places.

# Heart of Africa

by
Loren Lockner

Manufactured in the United States of America

ISBN No: 9781521769416

# *Prologue*

*The unmerciful sun refused my commands and set*
unconcernedly behind the dry acacias, stealing with it any
remaining warmth of the day. I lay curled in a tight ball, my left
cheek ragged and torn from an unrepentant thorn tree, my hands
clasped between trembling legs in a fruitless effort to stay warm.
The burrow was neither adequate for a bitter winter's night, nor
comfortable. I shivered in my filthy sweatshirt, hair full of
stickers and trash and who knows what else. I wept
uncontrollably, my situation so desperate that hope seemed as
elusive as rescue. Dreadfully hungry, alone and chilled, I
remained lost in the bush somewhere near the Limpopo River on
the vast wild border between Mozambique and South Africa.

Large black ants scurried into their warm holes constructed
from the sandy soil of this alluvial plain while the sharp, distant
cry of some hungry predator permeated the early evening air. I
had no such snug refuge and it was highly likely that before long,
my remains would be torn to shreds by hyenas, jackals and lions
while opportunistic vultures hopped in the distance, content to
wait for their share of the last tasty tidbits.

Useless salty tears stung my chapped lips and I knew I
needed to regain some measure of control and prepare a shelter
for the night. If I was cold now, at scarcely 5:00 p.m., what
would I be by midnight? Maybe, just maybe when dawn came, I

could find him—if he were still alive. I sobbed again at the possibility of his lying somewhere, mangled and torn, being ravaged by lions. Managing to pull myself upright, I scanned the dead winter veldt grass and froze in terror. The feline's evil eyes glowed yellow in the faint light, her tufts of pointed cinnamon ears tilted towards me. One lifted paw froze in mid-stride as her eyes widened in hungry interest. I played a transfixed staring game with the ravenous predator and wondered how it had all come to this.

# Chapter 1

## Before

*The airport whirled in complete chaos and I cringed* inside, abhorring anything akin to commotion and frenzy. My heart felt frozen, unable to thaw, even as this great, reviving adventure stared me in the face. I noted a young couple hurrying past, arms linked and laughing together in perfect harmony, and I stifled a sob. How could I ever love again? Had the shattered prequel to this trip been my last chance at happiness? Was I destined to become a bitter old maid, dulled by loss and crippled by love's desertion?

Eyeing the swirling masses in a kind of numb sorrow coupled with anxiety, I plunked my carry-on bag in the queue and waited nervously, occasionally glancing at my steel wristwatch as the Delta check-in line crept toward the open counters. At last, only one other individual fidgeted ahead of me; a frumpish middle-aged lady who riffled her bag, searching for misplaced tickets as the airline agent waited stoically for her approach. Thoroughly rattled, I fretted at the delay.

I was about to nudge the sluggish lady in front of me in an effort to urge her forward when I saw my mother maneuvering her way through the surging multitude. Mom's perfectly coiffed auburn hair gleamed dully as she skirted the line and joined me at the front of the queue. Dropping her leather handbag with an exasperated thump, she peered up at my distraught face.

"Don't you just hate airports? So you've been waiting all this time? I could have driven home and back, not just used the restroom—oh look, Mandy, there's one open." She gave me a small shove.

"Thank God," I muttered, leaning my carry-on against the gray paneling of the ticket booth.

"Good morning," said the efficient-looking agent, whose stiffly-pressed suit bore a tag embossed with the name Heather Jones.

"Good morning," I returned meekly. "I'm flying business class to Cape Town via Atlanta. I'd like an aisle seat if it's available."

"No window?" murmured my mother, knowing full well how much I disliked heights. Unfortunately, I could only fly if situated away from the porthole window, a fruitless effort to delude myself that the aircraft wasn't really held up by little more than air currents.

"Please, Mom," I begged and handed over my ticket and passport.

"An aisle seat is no problem for Orlando to Atlanta, since seating is wide open, but let me check your second leg. You're in luck, Ms. Phillips; we have a couple of aisle seats available upstairs near the front. Will one of those be alright?"

"Yes, thanks so much." I took a relieved breath which quickly turned to dismay as my mother jumped in.

"I'd like to point out the long line caused because there are only four clerks in attendance. With the exorbitant price of airline tickets these days, you'd think Delta could provide better service."

Ms. Jones straightened her shoulders. "Two more agents are on their way as we speak. Only the one bag?" Her plastic smile never wavered as she turned to me.

"Yes, and this carry-on," I said timidly.

"No problem. You'll need to affix this cabin tag to your bag before you board. I notice you requested a low-carbohydrate, low-fat meal with no beef or pork. The cabin crew will do their best to accommodate you."

"I certainly hope so," said Mrs. Phillips. "My daughter put in her request a good four weeks ago." My shoulders slumped at Mom's terse tones, but the airline agent seemed oblivious to my mother's rudeness.

Ms. Jones' fingers flew across the keys and within a matter of seconds, my boarding pass and passport slid across the counter. Mumbling my thanks, I moved away so the next customer could utilize the agent.

"Put the ticket and passport into your bag, Mandy. You'll drop it for sure. No, not that compartment—thieves know that *everyone* places their valuable documents in the outer pocket. There, for goodness sake!"

"Please, Mom! I'm not two anymore. I can take care of myself."

My mother gave an unladylike snort. "Oh, really? Considering the complete fiasco of the last three months, I sincerely have my doubts. My normally competent daughter has disappeared into thin air. It's like having a stranger for a child." I appeared to be in for another speech similar to the one I'd already received in the car, as if that hadn't been enough. My head began throbbing as I pulled the carry-on off to the side, my mother following.

"Mandy?" My mother's voice had taken on a different tone. "Are you sure you're alright?"

Embarrassed, I shook my head and turned away. "I… I just need to get on the plane."

"Running away won't solve anything. That's what your cousin says and I agree with him wholeheartedly. Ken believes you're just… "

I interrupted her. "I'm not running away, Mom. I need a vacation. Could you please just let me go on one without lecturing, belittling, or showering me with endless instructions?"

"I don't do that!" My mother retorted, stung.

"Yes, you do. You and Ken, each and every moment of every day." I turned an anguished face to my mother, who gasped at the despair she saw there.

"Oh sweetie… "

"You've both got to let me do something on my own. I *need* this vacation. I *need* to get away from the hell my life has become. I recognize you don't want me to go to Africa, but I have to. For myself! I need to find out if a competent woman can rise up from the ashes of what just happened to me. I'm twenty-nine years old and it's time for Mandy Phillips to start over."

I grabbed the carry-on and plowed ahead, seeking the security gate, my now-silent mother trailing behind me. The airport's loudspeaker droned its mandatory announcement regarding keeping track of bags and accepting no packages from strangers, as memories from three months earlier flooded back and threatened to overwhelm me.

# Chapter 2

## May, 2012

*The sweaty construction worker fired up his drill and,*
leaning his ample frame against the hammer, chipped away at a
portion of sidewalk only fifteen feet from the front door of Azure
Travel, his belly shaking like Santa Claus jelly. I stood still,
needing to enter the trendy shop, but almost paralyzed because
*she* sat in Josh's cherry-red Porsche and preened. *She* was an
amazing ensemble of frosted blonde hair layered haphazardly;
endowed with *the* perfect nose, full Botox lips, and a spectacular
cleavage which I judged had only a one percent chance of being
really hers. And to think she had managed this monumental
achievement all by age nineteen.

I felt old at twenty-nine; unattractive and frowsy. And now,
here I was, forced to enter the travel agency before the eyes of
Josh's latest squeeze, to settle my account alongside my
disgruntled ex-fiancé. Squaring my shoulders, I carefully picked
my way through unearthed brick and concrete, the rhythm of the
jack-hammer rattling me even further while effectively

7

accelerating my already throbbing headache. But it was my money, after all, wasn't it? Hadn't I diligently saved and paid for half the African safari to Kenya for my now defunct honeymoon? It seemed one of the bitter ironies of life that I was to be granted the immense thrill of fidgeting next to Josh in embarrassed silence as our credit cards were refunded by the discreet African-American travel agent.

Josh was twiddling with his leather jacket's zipper as I walked through the glass doors. Upon seeing me, he gave an exasperated sigh that clearly illustrated his annoyance at my tardiness. Josh was the personification of every girl's dream, especially that of the frosted nymphet adjusting her make-up in his sports car. At thirty-one, with midnight hair and cobalt eyes, he was the perfect Ken to her dazzling Barbie. Joshua Mason had the potential to become a house pediatrician at Charity Medical sometime in the near future, and desperately needed an arm fixture that created the illusion he had won it all. I, Mandy Phillips, hadn't been such a trophy.

We stood in painful silence as the efficient travel agent readied the paperwork.

"Here you go," she said at last and I dutifully signed the refund slip as Josh studied me. I'd just come from the hairdresser and my short chestnut hair had been cut to a shoulder-length blunt angle that emphasized my high cheekbones and auburn highlights. As the accounts manager at the hospital where Josh interned, I earned twice as much as my ex-lover, though I'd always recognized that to be temporary.

"I was wondering," Josh began tentatively as the travel agent moved to the rear of the efficient office to finish up the bureaucratic pile of paperwork attached to the refund, "if you wouldn't mind returning my engagement ring?"

The ring in question was a stunning engagement band with a huge emerald-set 1.2 carat diamond, specifically ordered by him and half paid for by me. There was no way Josh could ever have afforded the pricey ring his up-and-coming reputation stipulated, so I had dutifully obliged, handing over my hard-earned funds as if every good fiancée was expected to help pay for her ring. The lovely accompanying wedding band consisted of fifteen good-sized diamonds set inside a heavy gold band. It was a stunner, just like him. I pretended to fish through my beige shoulder bag before handing him the small velvet container. I'd rehearsed the whole tawdry scene several times over in my mind, and felt ready for him.

"You may have the wedding ring, Josh. I think you should get enough from the refund to present your juvenile playmate with a nice little trinket. However, the engagement ring remains mine. I'll consider it partial payment for all the money I invested helping *you* through med school over the last two years. You proved quite an expensive roommate."

Josh peered sideways at me, obviously shocked, having never heard me utter anything that assertive before.

He cleared his throat and whispered huskily, "It's just customary to return the ring, Mandy."

"I paid for half of it; I want half the cost back," I croaked. It was the moment of truth. Would I stand up or wimp out like I usually did in the face of confrontation?

I'd already canceled our joint credit cards and removed my belongings earlier that week from the small contemporary flat we'd shared. Josh actually had the gall to appear hurt. My cheeks suddenly burned at the memory of returning home early from an evening shift to find Josh and Stacy engaged in energetic fellatio upon my Scotchgarded lounge suite.

"Well, Mandy, if you feel that way."

"I do. I've applied for a transfer to St. Anthony's. We won't ever have to see each other again."

"Perhaps if you'd… "

"Perhaps if I'd what?" I whispered, barely able to look at him.

"Been a little more assertive like this from the beginning. I kept hoping you'd break away from your mother and cousin and become your own person. But Eva, and even Ken for that matter, was everywhere. In our kitchen, in our jobs, in our bed, for crying out loud. I couldn't handle it. I didn't want to hurt you, but I needed something different… something else."

"Well, you've got it now. A very *young* something else."

"She's young, but believe it or not, Stacy's more confident and independent than you. I have a word of advice for you—get away from your family, Mandy. Find out who *you* are. Because if you don't, you won't have anything to offer someone else."

I felt so humiliated, I couldn't respond.

Ms. Raymond returned with our credit card refund and quietly handed it over. She had apparently learned, after many years in the travel business, to be the height of discretion. The reading glasses perched above her nose magnified her already highly perceptive eyes, and I hated the fact that she'd been witness to Josh's speech. Could it only have been three months ago that two young lovers had fidgeted happily before her as they'd planned their dream honeymoon?

"Goodbye," I managed to choke out.

Josh flashed me what could be interpreted as an apologetic glance before hurrying out of the agency, the small refund slip waving in his fingers. I heard his Porsche rev and turned to watch him veer out of his lane with a screech and terrific jerk of the wheel. Ms. Raymond appeared strained and extremely uncomfortable.

"Free at last," I said, trying to smile. The middle-aged woman didn't smile back.

"Is there… is there anything else I can do for you, Ms. Phillips?"

"No, thank you." I turned to leave, the jackhammer still pounding the broken pavement. A rack full of colorful brochures hung near the exit, and my tired eyes gravitated toward them.

Ms. Raymond eyed me pointedly. "It's really a shame you *can't* go. Africa is one of the few destinations left where real adventure still beckons. I visited Tanzania and Zanzibar just two summers ago. Both proved to be truly fascinating places and *completely* different than the US. The pace is altogether slower, the skies bluer and the people, though unfamiliar, wonderfully intriguing. Of course, I could whip you up a safe little trip to Scandinavia or something."

And there it stood, her not-so-subtle statement branding Ms. Mandy Phillips as the quivering coward she really was. Now, Ms. Tanika Raymond patiently waited for me to renege on an African trip as I salivated over a European holiday in the fiords. My battered pride, coupled with a sudden, desperate urge to stand up for once, made me lift my chin.

"Quite the contrary. I wish to book a trip to Africa, but not to Kenya. Perhaps you could recommend a destination full of intriguing sights and wild animals? A first-class safari to… um… somewhere else?"

Ms. Raymond seemed momentarily taken aback, never dreaming I had it in me. "In… in *Africa*?"

"Yes. I have a three-week holiday coming up in six weeks and a pretty good-sized refund burning a hole in my pocket.

There's no use crying over rotten eggs. I *really* need to get away for a while, and Africa's where I want to go. Any recommendations?"

A strange expression flitted over Ms. Raymond's face. "I think I just might. A guided tour, or do you want to go it alone?"

Right now the *alone* word sounded irresistible to me. "Alone," I answered stoutly even though I was perfectly awful at all that alone stuff.

"South Africa is one of the most affordable African destinations right now and has a superb infrastructure. I can offer you a flight and a package at a far more reasonable rate than your honeymoon trip, and you can still travel first class. The animals are unsurpassed in abundance and variety. South Africa has been a front-runner in the preservation of endangered animals such as the rhino and wild dog. It's a fascinating place. However, there *is* a downside: motorists drive on the left and the crime rate is quite high."

I hesitated for only a few seconds. I had been mugged, my wallet stolen at gunpoint, on a holiday trip to Miami two years ago, and while it had taken months to get over *that* experience, I was not about to let Ms. Raymond sense my jitters.

I insisted stoutly, "I can deal with that. Just make sure you reserve me an automatic along with a great map, and book me into no less than four-star hotels. I don't do roughing it or drop-pit toilets, and I absolutely refuse to start any day without my coffee, a hot shower, and a neatly folded newspaper." I smiled broadly, suddenly happier than I'd been in months.

The travel agent grinned back. "I'll bear that in mind." And she added, "He's no great loss. Men like him are a dime a dozen. You deserve better."

Within twenty-four hours, Ms. Raymond called with *the* package for me, consisting of an adventure-packed fly/drive fourteen-day holiday. First, I would stop in Cape Town for a night, and then fly to Kruger National Park the next morning. After nine days on a self-drive safari in an animal-proof 4 x 4, I would zoom back to Cape Town to "bask in luxury," as Ms. Raymond put it.

"It's a long haul to Cape Town and since you'll arrive in the late afternoon, I think it best to book you into one of my other client's favorite hotels for the night. We'll use the same hotel when you fly back at the end of your trip. Charles travels a great deal and always stays at The Vineyard. Would you like to rent a car for your overnight in Cape Town, or just catch a taxi to the hotel and its surrounds?"

I gulped, glad Ms. Raymond couldn't see me on her end of the line. The urge to scream out *taxi* nearly won, but instead I answered confidently, as if it didn't matter a whit.

"A rental car please." It was clear I'd need lots of practice if destined to drive through a game park all by myself.

"Fine. I'll take care of it. I've placed you on an early flight the next morning up to Phalaborwa Airstrip, where you will pick up your second rental car. I booked you a luxury BMW for the first leg and a jeep for the second. From Phalaborwa you'll proceed to Letaba, a large camp inside Kruger National Park. I could send you to a private game reserve like Mala Mala, but they are more *couple*-oriented. This way you can venture out on your own but still vacation at a very high standard. Winter is the best time in Kruger for game viewing, so I've slotted you into three of my previous clients' favorite camps in hopes that you'll be exposed to several different eco-regions to glimpse the greatest variety of animals; though I'm afraid I might not be able to promise you the folded newspaper."

Humor and something akin to defiant challenge registered in her voice.

"I can survive without the paper," I laughed.

There was no time to reevaluate my decision. I was going, and that was that. I took Ms. Raymond's advice about warm clothes as well as leaving some space in my luggage for a few of the country's renowned African crafts. That very afternoon, realizing I'd need extra spending money, I ventured tentatively into the jewelry store where Josh had purchased the rings. Marvin's Jewelers was reluctant but cordial.

"No chance of you two making up?" Marvin asked. He looked to be about a hundred and had owned the shop forever. His fidgety blue eyes gleamed under gigantic black eyebrows that sprouted in a horrific cluster above his all-seeing eyes. I could tell he was a hopeless romantic.

"Not a chance," I replied firmly.

"Could I interest you in something else—a lovely diamond bracelet perhaps? That would make you forget him."

"Thanks Marvin, but no thanks."

The jeweler could see that no amount of urging was going to make me part with my refund and regretfully, shaking his shaggy head, he started the paperwork. Ten minutes later I gratefully walked out of his store with a balance of $3439.84 credited to my account. Now, that was service and then some.

# Chapter 3

*I was brought back to the present by my mother's voice.* "I worry about you embarking on this trip so much Mandy because, generally, you're not very… "

"Confident?"

"Well, that too, but it wasn't precisely the word I was looking for. Adventurous is much more, well, apropos. Let's face it Mandy, you'd prefer staying home and renting a DVD, for God's sake. Watching others deal with the hassles of life is much more your style. Even as a child you were an observer, not a joiner. Peace and quiet amidst unchanging routine is how you best cope with the stresses of life. You're so timid and grounded in routine that I guarantee you'll be miserable within a day. And God knows you hate dirt!

I sincerely don't know how you're going to survive in primitive Africa. I just hope they have indoor toilets! Remember how, during that trip to Memphis when you were a little girl, there was a long stretch without a gas station and Dad suggested you go in the bushes. My God, girl, you were in agony for fifty miles because you refused to squat in the weeds!"

"How sweet of you to remind me of that Mom, but you needn't worry. My travel agent has booked me into luxury hotels and promises me that the infrastructure in South Africa is practically first world."

"Practically? What on earth does that mean? You don't do *practically!"*

"Please Mother, keep it down!"

My mother didn't bat an eyelash. "I hope that Ms. Raymond at Azure Travel knows what she is doing. Oh, it's just too bad your marriage didn't work out. A good man and the start to a family is really what you need, not a trip to the heart of the third world."

We had arrived at Security and my mother, ticketless, would have to remain behind. Thank God for small favors! My mother just didn't get it. A man wasn't the simple cure-all for life's problems.

"Meeting the right man will change your mind about marriage, you'll see. Josh just wasn't the right man," Mom continued.

It was useless to argue with her, so I tried a different tactic. "You have to admit, Mom, that I need to get away. My life is just too ordered, too ordinary, and too awful. But you're right about one thing. I *have* created this tightly-organized pattern of existence that allows me to function normally, but there has to be more to life than a job, taxes, and a cheating fiancé. I need to expand my horizons and try, just this once, to carve out my own niche without anyone else's influence or interference. Goodbye, Mom. I'll see you and Ken when I get back with lots of great adventures to tell."

My mother choked down whatever she had meant to say and instead leaned forward to give me a quick hug.

"Be safe, Mandy. And you will... write?"

I smiled, amazed to note that Mother's eyes were actually tearing up. "I asked for first-class hotels. I'm sure they'll have Internet. I'll e-mail. I promise."

"Well then, goodbye, dear. Be safe. I worry about you so. I'll... I'll miss you."

"Don't you worry, Mom. I'll play it safe. Look, I've gotta go. Love you."

Gratefully, I kissed my mother's cheek and proceeded through Security without a glance behind me, all set for my grand adventure.

# Chapter 4

*Loneliness gripped me on that long flight to Cape Town* and I fidgeted, struggling to cope for at least ninety minutes before mercifully falling asleep in that semi-reclined position business class allows. Later, when I awoke, groggy and confused by my whereabouts, I was pleased to discover I'd slept a full six hours and now felt mildly refreshed. Bored, I flicked through the channels of my private TV before switching to the audio channels, settling on classical music. This seemed a good time to study the expensive guide book I'd purchased in Orlando regarding South Africa.

It appeared the fledgling democracy, not even twenty-five years old, was now a tourist haven. For over an hour I read about the country's diverse wildlife and culture, only flinching once at a section devoted to tips for the first-time traveler. My shoulders instantly stiffened, my palms grew damp, and the threat of one of my ever-lurking migraines began teasing my skull.

*For North American and European travelers, it is*
*important to note that South Africa and its*

*neighbors have adopted the British style of driving, so be prepared to keep to the left whilst driving. Local petrol stations are quite helpful, and don't forget to tip the attendant who puts gas in your car.*

There, in the muted light of the business-class compartment, I admitted how much I really hated to drive. Mandy Phillips was one who'd always be content to take the bus, hitch rides, or sit in the backseat with friends, happily denouncing all future car payments.

Now, I'd actually had the audacity to rent a car in a foreign country. Not only would I have to do all the driving, but that foolhardy decision would sorely test my lack of directional sense and recurring tendency to get lost. I'd always gratefully relegated the driving to Josh while he, the eternal show-off, had loved to parade his bright red Porsche through downtown Orlando.

The compartment lights intensified as the pilot announced that we were less than two hours away from Cape Town. A light snack of braised chicken, bean salad, and an untouched pudding managed to fortify me, and I breathed easier. Stay calm, I kept repeating to myself.

The descent into Cape Town was nothing less than spectacular. I pretended to appreciate it while white-knuckling my seat's narrow arms. At two in the afternoon, Table Mountain seemed bathed in light, its flat top reminding me of a marine haircut. The aircraft landed with a bump and a jerk, the noisy brakes quickly slowing the huge Boeing to a manageable speed until finally, we were being towed into the waiting port. I flexed my stiff fingers shakily, hesitant to unbuckle my seatbelt.

I nervously gathered up my things—the shoulder tote bag made heavy with an unread paperback and all the medicines my mother had forced me to pack—and prepared to disembark. Adding to its weight and waiting for use was a brand-new digital Nikon with a telephoto lens.

Twenty minutes later, with a South African stamp permanently printed inside my passport; I analyzed the long line of car rental agencies flanking the terminal before locating the one I'd booked with. A busy Cape Malay woman nodded briskly at me over the counter and with little conversation, set me up with a luxury car. She instructed me to head to the lot to pick up number B8, after inquiring whether I wished to rent a cell phone.

I shook my head. Who did I have to call, after all? I headed for the nearly-empty lot where an ebony-colored man with the improbable name of Precious pinned upon his shirt materialized at my shoulder. I handed him my card and was led to a beautifully clean, blue BMW with a CD player and unnecessary air conditioner. Precious examined the car, searching for any dents or scratches. I had asked the desk attendant for a map and now opened it for him, mentioning I'd booked at the Vineyard Hotel.

"Oh it's easy, Mama," soothed Precious. "You simply follow this road. Turn left at the robot, then left again and follow the signs to the N2, hey. Keep on until you hit the M3. It will be a lovely treed road, quite beautiful at this time of day, and keep going until you see a petrol station on your left. That is Paradise Road. Follow it and take the left road when the main road veers, which is Colinton Road. You can't miss the hotel. It's right here on the map." He whipped out a pen and circled the spot.

It sounded simple. Any *fool* could make it to the suburbs of Newlands and the Vineyard Hotel.

"Thank you," I said.

"It's a pleasure."

"Uh… Precious. That's an unusual name."

He wagged his dark head. "My mother gave birth to three sons who died within twenty-four hours after birth. When I was born and survived past the third day, she named me Precious. My *umama* was quite grateful for sure."

I smiled and offered him a tentative five-rand tip before grasping the proffered keys and swinging into the right side of the car. Taking a deep breath, I turned the key in the ignition but nothing, not even a whisper of the engine.

"I'm afraid you must press the button on the key, ma'am," instructed Precious politely.

"What?" I searched the dashboard, reddening.

"No ma'am, it's on the key." There it was, of course. I was too used to my keyless Prius. In this security-minded country, all cars were wisely alarmed. I sheepishly pressed the button and was immediately rewarded with an answering beep. The engine purred as I waved gratefully at the concerned attendant. Pressing the accelerator gingerly, I pulled out right into the oncoming traffic!

"*Leer bestuur, jou idioot!*" [1] Luckily the irate male driver of the red Audi managed to slam on his brakes in time, his pudgy hands pounding the horn.

Precious shouted frantically, "You must stay *left*, Mama! Look right! Remember—stay *left*, look right!"

I crawled into the correct lane as the fuming man flipped me the bird. My palms, sliding awkwardly over the steering wheel, were completely soaked and my heart was practicing the rumba.

---

[1] Learn to drive, you idiot! (Afrikaans)

Inching carefully down the road, my face burned. What little confidence I'd drummed up before the trip was completely blown. Precious had said turn left at the robot... robot? That meant traffic light, didn't it? Already confused, I decided to follow the other vehicles merging into my lane, hoping they'd lead to the exit.

Before I knew it I'd merged onto a highway clearly labeled the N2, and I breathed easier. Why, this was a piece of cake. As long as I followed other cars I'd be fine; within a few minutes or so, hopefully by some sort of osmosis, I would absorb this backward kind of driving and fit right in. Struggling, I created a little chant in my mind and repeated it over and over. *Stay left, look right, and everything will be alright.*

I proceeded a long way on the highway, noting plenty of off-ramps named with various letters and numbers such as the M7 and M5. The hotel was about fifteen kilometers away, which I translated to be about ten miles. If I kept this pace, I'd be just fine. A car swerved angrily by and it was only then I realized I was inadvertently traveling in the fast lane. Quickly moving to the left, I mentally thanked the slow-moving van preceding me. Situated behind its plodding pace, I could present a hazard to no one.

An overhead sign indicated the M3 coming up in five hundred meters. Meters! What in the heck did that mean? Confused, I realized it was crucial to connect with the M3 and took the first left. Within sixty seconds my mistake became apparent and I banged my fist upon the steering wheel in frustration. I'd exited too soon. Meters were like yards, only a couple of inches longer! I was supposed to exit at about five hundred yards, not fifty! Athletically perspiring, I frantically peered about and noted a green sign stating *M4* in bold, black letters. I'd taken the wrong turnoff and now was driving to who knows where on the wrong highway in a foreign country! Cursing as vividly as a trooper, I frantically searched for a place to turn around. My best bet was to exit at the first left, but after I did that I couldn't find the way back to the N2.

It's an embarrassing thing to acknowledge one's grossly evident faults. I remembered my clumsy dancing as a child and how I'd prayed that my nose would become more aquiline and less turned up, just like Joy Carter's. In high school, I had egoistically desired to tan better, wishing that the reddish shade giving my pale skin its only color would transform into an exotic tint. In even more vain moments I'd wished to sing like the lark and whisper like Marlene Dietrich. However, these faults, or perhaps flaws, were not truly embarrassing except at nude beaches or karaoke bars. But having a complete lack of direction—now *that* could be sticky!

Thank God I'd ventured out alone and had no one to comment acidly on my current mishap. I remembered rather belatedly how Josh had commented on my often faulty driving skills. Boy, would he have lots of ammunition now! After fifteen minutes of aimlessly turning right and left and getting nowhere, I finally pulled into a petrol station and asked how to return to the M3 heading for Newlands. The colored man, dyed a nutty shade of earth brown and missing half his teeth, kindly directed me back onto the highway, refusing my hastily-offered note.

Finally heading in the right direction, my eyes searched for Paradise Road and the gas station. Miraculously, it appeared and I veered left. Within half a kilometer the hotel emerged underneath a canopy of trees. The turn into the hotel's driveway loomed abruptly and I took it way too fast, screeching the tires as I braked. A less-than-stately entrance appeared just to my left, covered by an arched canopy and manned by a lanky uniformed attendant. As I brought the car to a jerky halt, a doorman named Mongi grinned, revealing a shiny gold tooth.

"*Sawubona!* Welcome! Shall I park your car for you, ma'am?" he offered. Too exhausted and embarrassed to do anything but acquiesce, I dropped the sweaty keys into his brown hand.

"You'll leave the keys at the desk?"

"Of course, ma'am."

I followed the porter inside, who wisely said nothing. To my surprise, the foyer and lobby were stunning, decorated in that quiet elegance which insists that one abandon their troubles at the door. Dual greenish-bronze, petite cannons pointed outward, guarding the marbled entryway, which opened into a deluxe foyer across from a large, sunny, atrium-styled restaurant. The hotel was well maintained, stylish, and exceptionally designed, with a fine sense of character and understated sophistication.

A tall, sandy-headed man leaned against a pillar near the entrance and had clearly witnessed my less-than-sophisticated arrival. His tired face, though sporting an unshaven chin, was highly pleasing with intelligent, chocolate-brown eyes above a thin nose within a highly tanned face. Laugh lines edged his mouth and he was casually dressed in safari gear. The stranger surveyed me unnervingly before suddenly smiling and I dropped my eyes, flaming once again.

I turned right and headed toward reception. A broad-shouldered, good-looking blond man bearing a name tag emblazoned with the frightfully long name of Reggie Maarschalkerweerd waited behind the beautifully polished counter, and flashed me a perfect smile. I shuffled through my bag to retrieve my hotel voucher and was rewarded with perfect professionalism. There were no mishaps, no confusion, no foul-ups. My reservation filled the computer screen; my name was even spelled correctly. Relieved to realize I was so clearly expected and welcome, I scribbled my passport details inside the small white boxes of the check-in form as the efficient male receptionist pushed the computer keys in tandem.

"Smoking or non-smoking?" Reggie inquired in a faint Afrikaans accent.

"Non-smoking please."

"I can arrange that, ma'am."

"I'm so very tired. Do you have a quiet section?"

"Yes, Miss Phillips. This is quite an old hotel, and unlike the new, thrown-up structures, the walls are thick enough to guarantee complete privacy."

I flashed him an exhausted smile. "And dinner is served when?"

"At seven onto ten. Shall I book you?"

"I'm not sure," I said truthfully. "Can I have a meal without a reservation, if I feel up to it?

"I'm sure that won't be a problem, Miss Phillips." Reggie motioned to a heavy black man in a maroon uniform to carry up my single bag.

"It has wheels," I informed the perspiring man softly as he grunted under the weight. The brightly clad porter took off, totally ignoring the wheels, with me following in his wake.

The tall, leaning man with the tired face grinned, noting the porter's progress.

"It's a better workout for sure," he said, his South African accent strong.

"It is indeed," I returned, trying to appear nonchalant.

The stranger shouldered a large, tan duffle bag and followed me out of the lobby and down to a cross-section of corridors. I made a show of checking out my room numbers and paused, genuinely bewildered.

He kindly leaned over and squinted at my room number. "This hotel used to be a house and therefore it is a bit of a maze. You must proceed down that wing and then up the short flight of stairs. Your room should be just… ah, on the left, I believe. You'll have a view of Table Mountain. Have a delightful stay," he added with a polite wave before turning left towards a different hallway.

"Thanks very much," I said and flustered, hurried down the corridor and climbed the four steps that led to my hall, wishing that I'd at least asked his name.

# Chapter 5

*I was far too weary to completely appreciate the mellow* uniqueness of the Vineyard Hotel that afternoon. I found the sweaty but cheery porter waiting by my second-story room that supposedly overlooked the mountain. Unfortunately, a heavy cloud cover blanketed Table Mountain and its surrounding environs, and I could barely discern the hill happily pointed out to me by the proud African. I was half-tempted to ask him about the tall stranger who had directed me to my room, but refrained, shyness winning over curiosity. Tipping the porter ten rand, I rapidly closed the door. The sandy-haired man must be another guest I'd unlikely encounter again, since I was leaving so early the next morning. Still, he had been very pleasant to look at, the soothing tones of his strong accent tantalizing. Pushing him out of my mind, I examined the lovely room.

It was spacious and lovely with a modern bathroom and wide bed covered in Monet colors. A huge window overlooked a wide garden where large brown birds waddled. I gazed for a long moment out of the window. The garden breathed lovely tranquility and I felt myself relaxing, the tension easing from my shoulders.

After a long, cool sponge bath I removed my shoes from my aching and slightly swollen feet and stretched out on the impressionistically-splattered spread. I fell asleep instantly, only to be awakened much later by loud, boisterous honking.

Frightened, I jerked upright. What in heaven's name was I doing sprawled across this unfamiliar, wide bed? Glancing frantically at my steel wristwatch, which I'd adjusted to Central African Time on the plane, I discovered it read 6:20. Was that p.m.? Rushing to the window, I threw back the curtains. Evening had settled in, overshadowing yellow-barked trees which sprang from low shrubs. Some kind of brown waterfowl strutted through the lush garden, making an appalling noise.

A few minutes later, after searching the room, I discovered a brochure entitled "Garden Birds of the Vineyard Hotel." Returning to the window, the disturber of the peace was quickly identified as an Egyptian goose. Noisy and conspicuous, the loud clacking and honking that denotes the species filled the early evening air. Moving away from the window, I realized I was starving. After a quick shower and fresh clothes, at precisely 7:00 p.m., I slid the flat card key into my pocket and ventured downstairs.

The hotel had two restaurants to offer. The first, a French restaurant called the Au Jardin, listed prices expensive even by South African standards. I instantly realized this was out, since I wouldn't be able to sit in its white table-clothed interior and feel comfortable alone. Restaurants like that bespoke of romance, as hushed whispers amidst the low lights, planned nighttime encounters. That simply wouldn't do, so I wandered into the warm light of the Courtyard Restaurant. A short, heavy woman with pleasant features led me across the patio through a maze of healthy plants.

I was amazed at how luxurious this hotel and restaurant really were, as the entryway had seemed so unassuming. A high-slanted sunroof let in faint glimmers of moonlight while a pebbled, blue-tiled fountain built in five tiers gurgled against the wall. The soothing sound muffled the eager chatter and plate-clanking of the few early patrons. Huge clay pots housed giant figs; nearby, tall, slender-trunked palms reached for the dim light of the beckoning ceiling, through which a three-quarter moon struggled to become whole.

Even the pillars holding up the wrought-iron walkway were painted muted green, their stripes causing the supports to resemble slender palm tree trunks. I appreciated the quiet harmony and understated elegance among the ample foliage.

Basking in my solitude, so pleasantly distant from well-meaning friends and critical family members, I felt myself truly relaxing in spite of my high-strung nature, and was suddenly glad I'd come. After ordering swordfish kebobs with a side salad, I opened the book I'd grabbed from the narrow sill across from my bed. Browsing inside the covers of *The History of the Vineyard*, I discovered the hotel was originally built around 1798 by the clever wife of Andrew Bernard.

An apologetic sound issued from somewhere near my shoulder. Believing it to be the waitress, I glanced up from the intriguing book and gasped. The slim South African from earlier in the afternoon stood before me, now smartly dressed in pressed gray linen slacks and a somber pinstriped shirt, his chin stubble-free.

"Is this seat taken?"

My heart beating wildly, I realized it was the moment of truth. Did I rudely order him away, or allow him to sit down? The old Mandy would have mumbled a quick, repelling response. But this was the new Mandy. "No, it isn't. Please sit down."

He eased his tall frame onto the cushioned seat and smiled warmly. "We haven't been formally introduced. My name is Peter Leigh. I'm a park ranger, environmentalist, and occasional guide. And you are…?"

"Amanda Phillips. Actually, Mandy. My job is nothing as exciting as yours, I'm afraid. Just an accounts manager at a local hospital in Orlando."

"An accountant? A noble and crucial profession. Maybe you can give me some insights on how to balance the numbers."

"The numbers?"

"Too much outflow and too little inflow from my accounts, I'm afraid," he said wryly.

"A common problem," I laughed.

The waitress returned, menu in hand. "You're eating with the lady, Mr. Leigh?"

"If she'll permit it." He cocked an eyebrow at me.

"Of course," I answered, surprised at myself.

Peter Leigh perused the menu. "I'll try the pasta tonight, Sophie. And a glass of red wine. House will do."

Sophie beamed and whisked away his menu.

Peter Leigh leaned back. "So, what brought you here to our lovely city?"

"A holiday," I answered nonchalantly. "I've always wanted to visit Africa and my travel agent recommended South Africa. Something about rustic charm mingled with first-world amenities."

"A very astute agent. Still, a long ways to come alone, isn't it?"

"I originally planned to travel with a friend, but they had another engagement and couldn't make it." It was so close to the truth that I hoped it would pacify the South African.

It apparently did, for he only asked, "And how do you like it so far?"

"What little I've seen is lovely. You must be proud of your city."

"I am. It is truly exceptional," he agreed, "but I have a bit of a confession to make. I'm actually just a visitor here as well. I stay at The Vineyard every time I venture to Cape Town, but I originally hailed from Zimbabwe."

"I just assumed you were South African."

"The accents are similar for sure, and I have lived in South Africa and Botswana for the past ten years, but I grew up in Harare."

"I've heard the situation is dire there," I stated, remembering what I had read about Mugabe and the country's insane inflation.

"Truly not a great place for man or beast. But I have found a new home in the north, near Kruger Park, and get to do what I love, which is work outside with animals and nature, so I have no complaints."

"'I'm heading for Kruger tomorrow," I said excitedly. "I'm venturing on a bit of a safari."

"Are you booked with a private game lodge or one of the public ones?" he asked, appearing genuinely interested.

"A public one, I guess. My first stop is at a camp called Letaba."

Peter Leigh flashed me a delighted smile. "That's a wonderful choice for the first-time visitor. Letaba is roughly in the middle of the park with lovely terrain, a fantastic view over the river, and loads of animals. You're in possession of a good camera I hope? Not just your smart phone?"

"Now, in that department, I'm prepared. I brought a Nikon with a telephoto lens. Cost me an arm and a leg, but I'm praying it's worth it." I suddenly felt very cheerful. This pleasant conversation with an attractive man made me feel younger and happier than I'd been in a long time. Maybe this would turn out to be a grand adventure and a tonic for my frazzled nerves after all.

Sophie arrived with Peter's red wine in one hand and a savory pasta dish in the other.

"Do you work in the park?" I asked as he sprinkled parmesan cheese on his pasta.

"Sometimes. I'm a private game guide and if I have a job, I take people through the park depending on their needs. Generally I concentrate on the northern reaches of the park, but I've worked all regions of the reserve. I conduct night drives, walking safaris, and guided jeep tours. But I also, because I'm a free agent associated with different travel bureaus, focus on the far north in Botswana. One of my specialties is the Okavango Delta, conducting boat tours. But, I'm off right now. Came down here to see my sister Elizabeth. She married a chap from Cape Town and works as a tour guide in Stellenbosch."

"The wine country?"

"That's right. She hosts day excursions to several of the better-known wineries on the route that include tasting, a gourmet meal, and an opportunity to meet the owners and visit their cellars."

I sipped my own delicious South African wine. "Sounds like a heavenly job."

"It is. Elizabeth lived in Namibia for about five years before moving to South Africa, so she speaks fluent German and Dutch. It's a good gig for her."

An inspiration hit me. "I'm returning to Cape Town for the last leg of my trip in about ten days. Do you think you could set me up with a wine tour?"

Peter grinned. "Your wish is my command. I'll call her tonight. Just give me a couple of dates so Elizabeth can organize something special for you. Maybe I could tag along and give her unwanted critiques about her guiding techniques."

"I'm sure your sister would appreciate that."

He laughed. "It would all be in good fun. Elizabeth's used to me ribbing her about whatnot."

"But won't you have a job yourself?"

"I'll be free at that time. I'll make certain of it."

Blushing, I quickly concentrated on my plate and devoured the remaining chunks of delicious fish while listening to Peter speak about Anne Bernard, the original owner of the hotel who, nothing less than adventurous, had left her native England with a husband twelve years her junior to man a post in the wilds of Africa.

"When Andrew took over the position of governor at the Cape of Good Hope, Anne's breeding and exceptional ability to adapt came in handy," stated Peter. "Feeling out of sorts with all the back-biting intrigue she discovered at Table Bay, Anne opted to build her own house, and look at what a house it turned out to be."

"She must have been an amazing woman to visit a wild country thousands of miles away from her home and not only survive, but prosper." I could only wish I were half so brave, and

I sighed. Finished with my dinner, I pushed my plate away, dabbing at my mouth with the white linen napkin provided.

Peter Leigh reached for the crystal salt shaker and peered at it as if were the most interesting accoutrement in the world.

"It's a brave thing to venture somewhere completely foreign and make a go of it. Brave indeed, particularly for a woman." He gazed directly at me, and a slight shiver trailed down my spine.

"You mentioned earlier that some of Anne Bernard's items are located in the gallery of the hotel?" How I managed to make the words come out so steady was beyond me.

"They are indeed. Would you like a gander?" He flagged down Sophie while I busied myself with signing the bill and then followed the tall guide, amazed at my burgeoning thoughts. I had rarely flirted or done anything unexpected in my life. I'd met Josh at a hospital function hosted by my boss and had stumbled into that relationship. Peter Leigh was definitely the most attractive man I'd met in ages, so why not…?

I spent the next fifteen minutes wandering the lovely expanse of the hotel, following Peter's well-modulated voice.

"Anne Bernard's touch is everywhere," he began. "The young woman was well-educated and not only kept an expansive journal of her time spent in Southern Africa, but also illustrated the pages with lovely pen-and-ink sketches. The hotel has dedicated this entire hall to excerpts of her diary. They make for fascinating reading." Peter Leigh paused as I examined some journal pages nestled inside lovely gold frames.

"She not only drew the natives, which were referred to by the Dutch as Hottentots, but also each and every person she'd had the fortune or misfortune to meet. Notice this ink sketch of fishermen near the shore. It reveals her special attention to detail.

One can only commend her. Unfortunately, it all ended tragically when her husband died prematurely."

"How so?" I asked.

Peter Leigh once again scrutinized me with his disconcerting brown eyes. "She was forced to vacate this beautiful city and country. Anne returned to the rainy isle, but this house, which she'd so lovingly designed, saw many subsequent owners from governors to generals, merchants to musicians. It wasn't until 1894 that the house was finally turned into a hotel, evolving into the quiet gem it is today."

"And that was tragic because...?"

"She remained husbandless in London, forced to forsake one of God's most beautiful cities. Drowned in her sorrows, I believe. Just like I figure you might be doing."

Stunned, I croaked out, "I beg your pardon?"

"It's apparent you've discerned the sun doesn't always shine every day."

"And how did you figure that out?" I returned coldly, feeling myself flame. We'd paused near the wide terrace overlooking the expansive garden.

"It's apparent you didn't plan to holiday in Africa *alone*. I can make out where you used to wear a ring. On your third finger..."

I glanced down. Though the white tan line where the magnificent ring once rested had faded; the circular white patch was still faintly apparent. My flush intensified as my stomach knotted.

I sputtered, "Thanks for the tour, Mr. Leigh. I have an early flight to Kruger tomorrow morning and need to get some rest. Thanks for your company at dinner and your informative tour of the hotel."

"Mandy…" Peter Leigh said, his chocolate-brown eyes suddenly remorseful.

"Good night," I managed before whirling and fleeing to the sanctity of my room.

Nestled wearily under the covers, a pile of used tissues littering the side table, I forced myself to reread the tour book carefully even though my eyes kept pooling. A drop splattered across the Stellenbosch page.

Angrily I slapped shut the book. Just who did Peter Leigh think he was anyway? Probably just some con artist targeting single women in hopes of either procuring a guide job or getting a quickie from what he believed was a lonely, forlorn woman.

"I am neither lonely nor forlorn!" I protested to the empty room. Did my pathetic face really reveal all that pent-up melancholy? Ruthlessly I snapped out the light, praying for sleep, but the happiness I'd momentarily felt over dinner dissipated as I wept into my pillow.

# Chapter 6

*The next morning I awoke bright and early to take a* long shower, hoping to revive myself. I hadn't slept well; Peter Leigh's words mocked me even in my dreams. I forced myself to check my packed bags once more before heading down for breakfast and there it was, a note in a white envelope slipped under the door. I waited a full minute before succumbing, and retrieved the small envelope. Peter Leigh's masculine, well-formed writing seemed just like him.

*Mandy,*

*I am so sorry to have caused you any distress.*
*That was a thoughtless comment on my part and I*
*hope you can forgive me. Perhaps I'll run into you*
*in Kruger and somehow make amends, but if not, I*
*wish you only the best on your travels. Be safe.*

*Peter Leigh*

I threw the letter into my carry-on and zipped the lid tightly. So much for a handsome diversion on the trip. Pathetic... that's what my life was... pathetic. I applied tear-disguising makeup and headed downstairs to take a meal of sunny-side-up eggs, brown bread, and some of the Cape's famous cheeses. I might as well have dined on cardboard.

Table Mountain glowed in the distance, rising out of the immaculately-manicured garden surrounding the picturesque hotel. Crane flowers, Egyptian geese, noisy waxbills, and a vivid double-collared sunbird vied for a final photo before I checked out. Peter Leigh didn't put in an appearance—not that I thought he would—and I resolutely drove the blue BMW to the airport and managed to drop it off without one single mishap. My mother, cousin, and Mr. Leigh for that matter, would have been astounded.

I relaxed in the sports bar for thirty minutes watching a drag race on the small screen and sipping an odd-flavored, warm drink called *rooibos* tea. The half-full South African Airlines flight to Johannesburg passed uneventfully and later, after a couple hours of fidgeting anxiously in the beautiful JHS airport, I finally heard the boarding call for my connecting flight to the Phalaborwa Airstrip.

I spotted the small aircraft outside the airport's huge windows and was suddenly filled with trepidation. A mere Jetstream—the blasted thing only held twenty-nine seats! Swallowing nervously, I boarded the compact plane and sank tentatively into my gray seat next to an obese black man whose eyes were already shut. No matter how I maneuvered, I couldn't distance myself from him and ended up sitting rigidly, my personal space cruelly violated as the last remnants of my self-confidence were vanquished.

The ensuing flight proved a nightmare as the toy plane bounced and groaned. The oblivious flight attendant handed out peanuts and soft drinks, never once spilling a drop during all the turbulence. The deafening throb of the twin propellers made it impossible to hold a conversation, much less think. I pretended to doze in my seat, squirreled away as far as I could manage from my sleeping neighbor, whose mouth now hung open. He snored gustily, though fortunately the din of the airplane motors drowned out the majority of his snorts.

Nearly two miserable hours later, after dosing myself with three antacid tablets and one of my migraine pills, the plane swung steeply downward. Through the small porthole I noted that the runway seemed far too short and gasped in horror. My seatmate snored on as I mentally measured the airstrip. No more than a thousand meters long or so, the small plane shuddered and lost altitude. Fiendish air currents battered the aircraft as its landing gear noisily descended.

I whispered a fervent prayer and prepared to die. Stomach in knots, I gripped the armrests until my knuckles turned white. The rotund gentleman next to me gave a loud snort as the plane touched earth and bounced twice.

"Are we there?" he mumbled groggily.

I was too frightened to do more than nod as the plane skidded to a stop. The perky flight attendant helped me gather up my things. Still shaky, I disembarked and peered about me.

The Phalaborwa airfield hosted a small but comfortable terminal and within minutes I'd retrieved my luggage (there were *some* advantages to small planes) and pondered my next move. My white shirt hopelessly creased and sweaty, I scanned the small line of rental car agencies. Surprisingly, all the major names were represented: National, Hertz, Eurocar, and Avis.

Heading toward the latter agency, I was rewarded when a bored young African woman handed me the jeep's key within a matter of minutes.

"An automatic, as you requested."

"Thanks. I'm spending the night at Letaba camp. Which way do I proceed?" I asked.

"Leave the airport and turn left. The main road runs right into the Phalaborwa Gate. Once inside, the signs will direct you to Letaba rest camp."

This sounded encouraging. "So it's just a few minutes away?"

The clerk gave an indolent shrug. "The gate is close, but once inside Kruger it's a bit of a ways to Letaba. I must warn you the road is bad in some places." She passed me an area map and focused upon the next customer; a thin, washed-out man wearing thick glasses. I'd been dismissed.

Tentatively I headed for the small parking lot and handed my car claim tag to a skinny black man in a blue jumpsuit. He pointed a finger at a sleek 4 x 4. The jeep gleamed jungle green, and came equipped with comfortable seats and a removable top for better game viewing. The languid attendant hauled my luggage into the spacious rear and showed me how to remove the roof before flashing me a lazy thumbs-up send off. Remembering my trial run in Cape Town, and chanting the little song of *stay left; look right,* I departed the minuscule airport for my grand safari. Over the next ninety minutes I spent my time alternating between avoiding potholes, lagging behind smoking trucks, and gazing amazed at the countless metal shacks situated just off the road.

A wire fence, decorated in breeze-filled plastic trash bags, surrounded a makeshift soccer field where shoeless ebony youths kicked at a dilapidated soccer ball. A large trash heap, attended by sturdy goats and a rooting pig, stood near a water pump where a long line of skinny girls in outgrown faded dresses waited for a turn. An old man leaning on a cane and dressed in a drab brown suit surveyed the road. A brand-new Toyota Land Cruiser sailed past my slower jeep, packed with a lively white family obviously heading for Kruger Park.

I passed a billboard decorated with the red curved and crossed ribbon symbolizing the fight against AIDS and a scrawny child of about five clad in a dirty pink dress, kicking at the dirt before waving energetically at me. I shyly waved back before gripping the steering wheel more tightly. Where, oh where was the gate?

By the time I made it to the Phalaborwa Gate, I felt exhausted and irritable. I'd expected Letaba to be close, but realized I still had a great distance to continue to reach my lodgings. To top it off, I had headache that was threatening to transform into a full-fledged migraine. I left the rental vehicle to pay the park entrance fee. Here the grounds, though roughly landscaped, were well-maintained. I was surprised when the smiling park attendant handed me a large paper bag.

"No plastic bags allowed in the park, ma'am." The young man grinned, a wide gap situated charmingly between his front teeth. His tag indicated the comforting name of Charles. He sold me a detailed map, stating, "Not to worry, ma'am. Letaba is due east on the H-9. Just follow the signs. You'll pass through the Rhidorda Pan, where one often sights giraffe and elephant."

My pulse quickened as I followed a white Mazda onto the tarred road. I had just handed the entry form to the green-uniformed guard, when I gasped and pointed out the window.

There, a large, graceful herd of brown and white buck, a few sporting twisted black horns, grazed tranquilly near the entrance.

The guard chuckled. "Impala, miss. There are thousands in the park. See their bottoms?"

I peered intently. A telltale *M* decorated each buck near its white, tucked tail.

"They're the McDonald's of the park. Everything wants a taste of those juicy hindquarters." I laughed merrily with him before heading toward my final destination of the day, my headache subsiding somewhat.

It was the afternoon of the giraffe as I set out for Letaba on the main road. My first glimpse of the world's tallest mammal came through the trees, where a stately head bobbed between thorny branches as it loped along. Too distant for a good photo, I parked the jeep so I could watch my first real sighting lurch out of view. Later, at a water hole, three of the large creatures drank, spreading their long legs wide apart so they could maneuver their oversized necks close enough to lap up the water. I just couldn't get enough of the amazing creatures. A few impala wandered between them, eyes briskly alert before dropping their lovely heads to drink. Large ground birds, speckled black and white, scurried between them to drink and chatter nosily. Within an hour at Kruger, I'd snapped over fifty photos.

I glimpsed little more the rest of the afternoon until noting the oddest tree I'd ever run across. Its monstrous squat trunk reached root-like tentacles toward the cobalt sky. I thumbed furiously through my guide book, making the victorious identification. It was the famous baobab, called the upside-down tree by locals. Often several thousand years old, during winter the baobab's leafless branches hover above its enormous trunk, gleaming an eerie gray-white in the bright sunlight. Impossible to miss, the tree's majestic starkness is nearly indescribable.

I took at least a dozen shots from every angle with the newly initiated Nikon, hoping to obtain one decent shot of the twenty-five meter high tree to blow up and frame for my new, bare-walled condo. Nearby, I noted an area blackened by brush fire, the haphazard path of flame having randomly missed several thorny trees while totally destroying others. I'd read on my initial flight to Cape Town about the veldt fires that redistributed the nutrients back into the parched earth during the winter. Their merciless flames enabled the wild grasses and flowers to spring forth with renewed life during the rainy season that started in October.

I traveled no faster than fifty kilometers an hour that afternoon and finally arrived at Letaba tired but relaxed, having for once thoroughly enjoyed driving.

Entering the large reception hall, I marveled at the handsome place and discovered the camp's name meant "river of sand" in Sotho, one of the many South African languages. Spectacularly situated above the sweeping, wide bends of the Letaba River, it overlooked a huge flood plain where unafraid animals drank and grazed upon the rich grass bordering the shallow water. After being allotted a small two-bed rondavel with a quaint thatched roof, I lugged my maroon bag to the small room overlooking the river. I halted, amazed. Only ten yards from my door, a small, sturdy buck lifted soft eyes to observe me. Fearless, it chewed on a sprig of bright grass hanging from its lips like a thin vegan cigarette.

The creature was lovely beyond measure with broad ears, bright, dark eyes, and a smattering of white spots dappling a lovely brown coat. Dainty black hoofs stepped gingerly over the green grass, artificially watered by a long length of black hose. I remained transfixed for several minutes until the unperturbed buck moved away. Later I discovered a huge glass information board inside the large, grassy area, discussing the prevalence of bushbuck inside the Letaba rest camp. Bushbuck were allowed to wander the enclosed grounds freely, though only females and their young are allotted this privilege. The bushbuck males were so reputedly fierce, they'd been known to attack lions and often emerge victorious, impaling the predator with their short, sharp horns.

Huge trees of Natal mahogany and exotic marula dotted the well-maintained lawn. The camp buzzed with bright yellow and black weaver birds busily snatching grass so they could intricately weave their basket-shaped nests. Iridescent blue-black starlings made my late afternoon snack of a grilled cheese and tomato sandwich a supreme pleasure as the cheeky birds tried to snatch crumbs off nearby tables. The self-service restaurant overlooked the immense river, delivering an unblemished view of more grazing impala, which were later joined by black- and brown-striped zebra. Confused, I flipped through my guide book, stunned that these South African zebra were nothing similar to the ones I'd ogled while visiting the zoo as a child. Even more distant, a large herd of wildebeest lazily made their way downriver. Lunch at the hospital cafeteria had never been like this!

Later, I returned to the reception hall to explore Letaba's elephant museum, which I'd noticed upon my arrival. Inside, huge tusks and skulls of the Magnificent Seven—elephants so named because of the immense size of their tusks—filled the hall. One display in particular fascinated me. The elephant Shawu had the longest tusks ever reported in the park. Each tusk measured over nine feet in length and hung on the white-washed walls in quiet dignity. Hopefully, I would be able to view some descendants of these large "tuskers" for myself over the next few days.

"Having a good time?" drawled a familiar cultured South African voice.

I whirled and there stood Peter Leigh, once again dressed in his safari khakis and now sporting a wide-brimmed hat.

"What are you doing here?" I hissed.

He shrugged. "Well, today I'm holidaying, though I'm supposed to meet a client here tomorrow. I often work in the park, remember. This museum is one of my favorites. Fancy running into you, though, Miss Phillips."

A family of Japanese tourists pushed by me, oblivious to my mounting anger.

"And you just *happened* to land in the very same camp, in the very same museum in the whole of Kruger Park, as me?"

"Strange, isn't it?" He nonchalantly turned away from my angry eyes and pointed at the sign below the huge tusks. "This is Shawu—an amazing tusker. It was a real shame when he died. You know that elephants have six sets of teeth and after they wear down the last one, they slowly starve to death."

"You need to get away from me," I ground out between clenched teeth.

"Ach, shame. Look Mandy, I'm sorry about last night. My sister swears I have an uncanny knack of saying just the wrong thing at the wrong time. My sincere apologies. I planned on telling you I was flying straight up to Letaba. Last night I was truly delighted to learn you were headed to the same camp as me. Please, please forgive my rudeness."

But I had already turned away, heading for the glass doors of the small museum. Peter Leigh caught up with me and gently took my arm to stop me exiting the small museum. His voice shook with emotion. "Alright, Mandy, you have to listen to me. I have a confession to make. I'm sure this is going to come as a bit of a shock to you, but you see, I'm actually your hired guide."

Flabbergasted, I stared blankly at him before sputtering, "Is that supposed to be some sort of pick-up line?"

"No, it's the God's honest truth." Peter fished inside his back pocket and handed me a creased paper. The document was an order form from Azure Travel.

I scanned the paper in disbelief. "The travel agency hired you? My agency from Orlando, Florida?

"Yes, via a Ms. Raymond, actually. It seems that the price she quoted you was guide-inclusive. It's clear she neglected to tell you that fact. I figured that out when you didn't recognize my name when I introduced myself to you last night at the hotel. You're the client I'm supposed to meet tomorrow."

"I remember very well my conversation with Ms. Raymond about the trip," I said indignantly, "and I can guarantee she mentioned nothing about my tour being 'guide inclusive.'"

Peter Leigh shrugged. "Then I guess you're just lucky she caught the mistake in time. Look, Mandy, the bottom line is that Kruger isn't a great place to be traveling alone. The park is the size of your state of Massachusetts and there are tons of twisty dirt roads, with hours between camps and toilet facilities. Have you thought about what you'd do if you got a flat, ran out of petro, or were charged by one of these big fellas here? There are dangers lurking in a wild place like this that most city folk can't fathom. It's better to have a guide if you're on your own. Particularly a pretty woman like you. Trust me."

His final words caught me off guard and I experienced that insistent telltale blush, exposing my deep-seated insecurities again. Dumbfounded, I was literally rendered speechless.

He continued, sensing my acute embarrassment. "I recognize that you really want to travel alone, but I'd feel much more at ease about it all if you'd just allow me to accompany you on your drive tomorrow. I'm used to driving a jeep, which I know was part of your tour package, and my assuming the wheel would enable you to enjoy the splendors of the park. I've been doing tours for nearly ten years and I'll not only give you insights on the flora and fauna inhabiting Kruger, but might even enable you to the catch the Big Five."

"The Big Five?" The question was out of my mouth before I could stop myself.

"Those are the big animals considered most dangerous for hunters. They're the lion, leopard, elephant, rhino, and Cape buffalo. Most visitors to the park pray they will run across a couple of them, though frankly, there are others creatures vastly more interesting."

I fidgeted as he spoke. The insulted part of me longed to tell the arrogant Zimbabwean to get lost, but the other, the more curious and vulnerable part, hankered to learn more about this incredible wilderness. And best yet, he would drive. What propelled me to agree, to this day I'll never fathom.

"The gate opens at 6:00 a.m.," I said sharply. "I'll meet you at the parking lot outside of the reception area near my jeep. You have one day to prove to me that you aren't wasting my precious holiday, Mr. Leigh."

"I'll be there." His words drifted after my rapidly departing figure. I couldn't flee fast enough.

One of the beauties of Letaba, I later discovered that chilly evening, were the benches overlooking the river. It was there in the fading light of the cooling evening that I glimpsed my first elephant. The massive herbivore sauntered down the sloping bank and drank gustily from the slow-flowing river. I watched the big fellow for over twenty minutes as the tusker took his own sweet time to drink, forage, and then drink again. By the time he lumbered back up the embankment, his huge footsteps deeply indenting the sand, the sun had finally disappeared. The sky slowly filled with an array of shining stars so clear and unblemished, it took my breath away.

I remained profoundly disturbed by the events of that afternoon. Ever since my encounter with Peter Leigh in the museum, I'd racked my brains about all my conversations with Azure Travel's agent. Then it hit me. Ms. Raymond had been witness to Josh's and my less-than-dignified encounter regarding our breakup. She had then hurriedly set me up on a trip to a country whose crime rate was notorious. It was likely Ms. Raymond had added on the services of a guide in belated penitence. Frankly, it didn't matter why Peter Leigh had intruded upon my trip; what mattered was how I handled it as the new, independent Mandy. Would my quest to become a more competent woman suffer from having a private tour guide? I finally concluded that giving Peter Leigh one day to prove himself a reliable guide might be the right course. Somewhat soothed by my choice, I contemplated dinner.

I ventured late that night into the restaurant and enjoyed a casserole of kudu stew, tasty bright orange butternut, and a delicious malva pudding for dessert. I tried an unfamiliar drink called Appletizer and found it refreshing and tasty as I unashamedly eavesdropped on the conversation of some loud and boisterous Australians who'd had a very productive day. In an accent impossible to misplace, they boasted of lucky and unexpected sightings. I listened intently, memorizing their references to locations in hopes that those selfsame animals would present themselves to me over the next few days.

"That cheetah," said a balding, muscular man who vaguely reminded me of Steve Irwin, "didn't have a scrap of fear!"

His mate, lanky and sandy-haired with a bristly three-day growth of beard, responded enthusiastically. "Did you see how he leaped right up onto the road marker, the sun directly behind him? It was a spectacular shot—one in a million."

"I just hope you focused the camera, Jeff," laughed a pixie-haired woman who might have been his girlfriend or wife. Tanned and slim, she wore shorts even at dinner.

"You bet I did," he protested toothily. "And that white rhino and her baby, I pray you got a good shot of her suckling at her mum."

"Of course, of course," chortled the first man. "I must say that I'm thoroughly chuffed. That Tsendze loop has proven a fine one."

Another woman, blonde and stout, exhibited a no-nonsense attitude in regards to her companions that designated her as the trip organizer. "Tomorrow will be a long day, Billy," she announced. "We must rise at the crack of dawn if we're going to make it to Punda Maria."

"Christ!" grumbled the first man. "It's a bloody shame we couldn't book a closer camp. We'll have to kill ourselves driving that far north in one day."

"It'll be worth it," stated the organizer firmly. "We'll see Crooks' Corner. And I plan to linger around until we rustle ourselves up a good posse of nyala. Jeff says he needs a full male head for his buck page. We were lucky to snap those roan and sable antelope. With the nyala, we'll have everything he asked for."

"Don't worry, Tracy. We've got three days there and I promise you'll have two hundred shots of nyala. They're supposed to be thick as impala near Pafuri."

I repeated the unfamiliar names under my breath. I'd have to check my map first thing back in the rondavel. The photographic team blustered and boasted loudly, enthusiastically drinking their way through the entire meal. Though alone at my solitary table, I had ample entertainment and didn't for one second allow myself to feel lonely, though more than once I wondered what my new guide Peter Leigh was up to.

Later, sitting Indian-style upon my single bed, the night imbuing the camp with wild and exotic sounds, I studied the map and planned my next day's route. I was booked for these first three nights in Letaba, a further two in Mopani, and a final pair in Shingwedzi which, according to the map, was situated not far from Zimbabwe. If I planned my trip correctly, I could make it as far north as Punda Maria during my last days in the park and visit the exotic Crooks' Corner I'd heard about at dinner. A guide book examination revealed how one could view three countries at once in the small triangulated area separating their borders.

Just before bed, I perused the two animal identification books I'd purchased, seeking to familiarize myself with the more common animals. I didn't wish to appear a complete idiot in front of Peter Leigh. With a sense of glee, I discovered the antelope my Australian dinner entertainment had spoken about. The beautiful nyala was notable because of its extremely hairy body balanced on pale, slender legs. The fascinating buck, dominated by wide white stripes and a strange bar of black across his nose, seemed beautiful beyond belief. His antlers, though not as spectacular as the magnificent kudu, made me as excited as those Australians to snap a shot.

A ruckus outside my rondavel brought me off the single bed and I cautiously opened the door. A shout from near the benches where I had sat earlier coaxed me from the room. A small, tight cluster of people hovered near the bench I'd vacated that very evening.

"Get back! Get back!" protested a burly black man clad in a green ranger's uniform.

I, of course, hurried forward, curiosity propelling me toward the shifting crowd. Fairly obedient, the group backed off a distance of two to three meters, watching the ranger bark into his walkie-talkie as he stood guard beside an upside-down bin. Suddenly Peter Leigh came at a run, clutching a large net and a snake stick. The first ranger gestured the crowd to back away and lifted the trash can whereupon a huge snake, curled and defensive, hissed and lunged. Peter Leigh jumped back and shoved the curved pole hard upon the angry snake's head. I gasped. No snake lover, this was the stuff of my worst nightmares.

"Nothing to worry about," said the boyish Peter Leigh calmly to the gathering crowd of onlookers. "It's just a baby, and a fine specimen at that."

A baby? The oversized thing was a mass of writhing scales.

"What is it?" I gasped as a plump Afrikaner lady near me backed away, obviously as nervous as I.

"Just a rock python," answered my guide, glancing up at me with a reassuring smile.

Apparently the fact that this constrictor might just as easily have slithered into my rondavel as the trash bin never occurred to anyone. I tensed as the two men tussled with the beast. All in all, the whole matter was handled quite professionally and quickly. The African ranger distracted the snake with his hands and stick while Peter Leigh deftly captured and bagged the infant. Though dubbed a baby, the two grown men were hard-pressed to carry the heavy eight-foot reptile away.

"It must have crawled up the embankment," observed a stout European tourist. "Dese electric fences can't keep 'em out."

The entire camp was encircled by a comforting length of electric fencing, designed to zap any unwanted wild visitor in a not-so-gentle reminder to stay on their side of the fence. Of course, any self-respecting snake could burrow or slither underneath the gaps where soil met fence. I gulped and backed away from the noisy proceedings. I hated snakes as much as any die-hard Indiana Jones fan. Ever since a nasty encounter with a curious cottonmouth that had found its way into my grandmother's swimming pool outside the Florida everglades, my love of swimming has been stifled somewhat. Still, the quiet confidence and expertise in which Peter Leigh had handled that snake comforted me immensely. Maybe having an experienced guide was prudent after all.

Upon returning to my room, I searched the entire length and breadth of that tiny space, paranoid beyond reason that the baby constrictor's sister may have slithered her way into the circular room. I didn't sleep well that night and it was Peter's Leigh's lean, competent face that soothed me into sleep.

# Chapter 7

*The next morning, after loading up with bread, cheese,* and fruit, as well as several liters of cold water, I trotted to where I'd parked the safari-green jeep under a shady tree to wait for Peter Leigh. Shrieking, I leaped back. A huge lizard, at least half a foot long, sat brooding upon the peeling tree trunk. Plump and covered in spiny scales, its blunt head and upper body glowed eerily aquamarine as he moodily observed me. Grabbing my camera, I moved closer. The reptile hissed, revealing a bright orange lining inside its mouth. I snapped the shot before darting back, afraid the temperamental reptile might launch itself from its perch and attack me with needle-sharp teeth.

I heard a male chuckle behind me. "He's a lot of show, that 'un." A stout Afrikaner in very tight beige shorts sagging below a rotund beer belly stroked his bushy mustache and chewed thoughtfully on a toothpick. "You got a good shot?"

"Yes… um… what is it?"

"Blue-headed tree agama. Likes to hang out in the camp and frighten the ladies. Actually has a nasty bite if you get too close. Lekker color, hey?"

I remembered the guide book's use of the word and smiled to show I understood. My new friend grinned, one front tooth protruding over the other. "Another neat lizard found around here is the rainbow rock skink. Got a dandy blue-striped tail. Not as scary as this one though. You here alone?" he asked nonchalantly.

I tensed. "No," I said firmly. "I have a guide. You?"

"Just traveling with some mates. Keep an eye out for pesky reptiles then." He gazed past me and added quickly, "A good day to you."

As he sauntered off, Peter chuckled behind me.

"Amazing specimens, those *lizards*. I'd watch out for their nasty bite."

"You're here on time, I see."

"I'm always punctual, milady. You sleep well?"

I stared up into his handsome, tanned face. He wore his brimmed hat and khakis, and held a fairly good-sized wicker basket in one hand and a rifle in the other. I wasn't sure I found the rifle comforting.

"I did find the snake a bit disturbing," I said. I had to check inside my rondavel to make sure a relative wasn't lurking inside."

"Wise decision. My brother-in-law always checks his shoes each time before donning them after he found a baby scorpion in one a few years back. You can't be too prepared." He lifted the rifle reassuringly. "You ready?"

"Yes."

"Then let's get out there and see what this lovely day has in store for us."

Peter preceded me to the dusky-green, six-passenger 4x4 and extended his hand for the rental key. "I hope you have a pullover?" he asked while opening the rear door and placing his rifle and gear inside.

"A sweatshirt? Yes, I do," I said. "Why? The weather is delightful."

"I want to remove the top, so if we have a sighting you can stand up and photograph whatever we find. The downside is it can get a bit chilly, particularly in the morning being winter. You okay with that?"

"Yes," I answered and opened the heavy right-hand door. I'd found that yesterday, despite its sturdiness, the game vehicle was amazingly comfortable. With plenty of leg room, the small compartment to my left was just perfect for my new camera and cold water.

"Then let's get this show on the road," said Peter, and with a roar and a jerk, we were off.


That morning we ventured off the paved roads, meandering east to follow the Letaba River. The terrain outside of Letaba camp consisted of low-rolling hills, parched dry; its resident trees were twisted and ghostly-looking, since the rains had not yet come. Peter drove parallel to the wide river for a long time, observing more of the tasty impala and stopping once to allow me to snap a shot of a group of five young males whose lovely horns dipped gracefully as they idly chewed on grass, unperturbed by my photo mania. Two black-and-buff striped zebras browsed in the distance, and a large, dark object off to my right just *had* to be an elephant. A really close shot of the pachyderm had, for now, eluded me, but I kept my camera cradled in my lap in high hopes.

The knobby hills leveled out into open, grassy plains dominated by the ever-present thorn trees. Peter parked the 4 x 4 after thirty minutes and gazed into the dry brush, using his binoculars.

"There," he pointed, handing me the glasses. "Wildebeest, but unfortunately we're not close enough for a good shot." I squinted through the strong glasses at the small herd. Though not the best shot, I took one anyway, pretending not to notice Peter's small smile.

"Do you know much about the history of the Park?" asked Peter, starting the jeep again.

"Not much. I only read the little blurb inside the map I purchased."

"The place is huge. It's almost 20,000 square kilometers or about 7,500 square miles. It has many different biomes and more game is concentrated in the South, though personally I prefer the north because of its more unique game and baobab trees. It became the Kruger National Park in 1926 after having been a preserve called Sabi. There's a private game park adjacent to this one called the Sabi Sands. Nice place, if you have a ton of money."

"It can't be nicer than this," I stated. "It's all so lovely."

The bush dominated the land like I'd always imagined Africa; wild and seemingly inhospitable, every species but man adapting to the harshness of the dry landscape.

An evil-eyed bird settled in the road before us and plucked at a large pile of droppings. Peter slowed the jeep and I rose through the roof opening to obtain a better view. The size of the dung pile was so massive that even I recognized it as belonging to an elephant. Heart quickening, my head jerked nervously side to side as I searched the dense brush for the large herbivore. Finally, convinced no elephant lurked nearby, I turned my sights back to the bird. His hooked banana-colored beak proved quite effective as he burrowed through the poo, his yellow eyes constantly alert.

"That fellow is the Yellow Hornbill. He has a loud, irritable cry, black-and-white plumage, and a long tail. The elephant dung is a few hours old and becoming dry, which means she's long gone, I'm afraid. It's when the dung is still smoking that you know a herd is near." Peter eased the jeep closer to the large pile of droppings and with an indignant squawk, the bird flew up and alighted in a nearby thorn tree.

I remained standing, protruding up through the roof, and just listened. Under the blue bowl of cloudless sky, the quiet of the bush was broken only by the distant cooing of some kind of dove. I stared at a black-and-white bird wagging its tail as it hopped through the shrub.

"That's an African pied wagtail," drifted up from Peter. "You like birds?"

"I love 'em," I replied. "So small and perfect. My grandfather was a birdwatcher and belonged to a walking club. He ventured out every Saturday on a hike to take photos of all the amazing birds of Florida. I accompanied him a few times before he got sick."

"Too many people ignore the lesser creatures. I'm pleased that someone else besides me enjoys them."

I glanced down at Peter. He leaned against his door, peering up at me, warmth seeping from his brown eyes. This time I didn't blush or turn away. Suddenly I realized that if I glimpsed nothing more during the duration of my trip than that little African pied wagtail hopping near our vehicle, it would be enough for me. I sank back down beside him, my breath catching as a slow smile suffused his handsome, tanned features. In mounting confusion, I made a pretense of scanning the bush again.

He idly changed gears and drove leisurely, relating facts about the park to me. "It used to be mostly accessible by train in the early '20s, but the government started building roads in the 1920s and '30s so the public could enjoy the park. Have you ever read *Jock of the Bushveld?*

"No," I answered.

"Pick up a copy of the classic novel in the store here at Letaba. It will give you great insights into the times before the park, when all was wild and untamed. Look there at nine o'clock," he added quietly.

A young coyote-like creature trotted by the road. Peter swung over to the side and I popped back up through the roof. "Can you get him in focus?" he asked.

I managed several shots before the lone dog dashed into the thick brush. "What was it?"

"A black-backed jackal. Lots of those fellas about here. They feed on rodents and hares, but also the leftover carrion after the bigger creatures have had their fill. And just there…"

His voice sounded casual enough, but I could discern a trace of excitement. The huge rhino lifted his massive head and stared straight at us, as if daring me to snap a photo. I focused and shot once, twice.

"There, look at the side of the road—the rutted mud and dug-out area," whispered Peter. "That's a rhino midden. The rhino sniffs the dung and adds to the pile. It's like a message station. All rhinos in the vicinity use it as a public toilet, so to speak, and learn who's wandering the neighborhood. It's a large one… that means there's quite a few white rhino about."

I adjusted the telephoto lens of the Nikon before snapping twenty more shots. The rhino just kept chewing, its small eyes examining us with as much interest as we did it.

"The white rhino isn't really white at all," Peter explained softly. "His Afrikaans name is actually derived from the wide lip he uses in grazing. The black rhino forages on brush and shrubs and therefore is hook-mouthed and much smaller in size. It's also much more aggressive. Unfortunately, both species are highly endangered."

The rhino, likely tired of all my photographic nonsense, trotted daintily back into the thick brush. I flopped back down into my seat and sighed blissfully.

"What a heavenly day. I just can't understand how anyone could kill those beautiful animals," I stated.

"They're heavily poached for their horns. The Asian market pays very well for their 'medicinal' properties. They're suspected to be a strong aphrodisiac. I imagine you're getting hungry. I know a great rest stop a few kilometers away where we can lunch."

The pristine rest stop came equipped with modern bathrooms tucked under shady marula trees. At a cluster of picnic benches I offered up my cheese and fruit while Peter pulled out the large picnic basket. He spread out a red-checkered tablecloth over the roughly hewn table. Black iridescent starlings hopped close by, hoping for spare crumbs from our delicious chicken salad sandwiches and hardboiled eggs. Chattering a few trees away, a trio of vervet monkeys twitched and sprang from limb to limb.

"If those infernal monkeys get too close, just give 'em a whack," said Peter, his eyes scanning the horizon. "I had one grab a potato out of my hand right before it was set to encounter the frying pan a few months back, while I led a walking trek in Chobe. Devious little devils they are."

"You love all this don't you?" I asked taking a bite of my now-shelled egg.

"I really can't imagine doing anything else. Everything is so connected here, so alive and vibrant. If a visitor is patient, not like some of our tourists, they can witness truly amazing sights."

"I'm patient," I stated quietly.

"I sense that." Peter stared a long while into my hazel eyes while a smile tugged at his deep laugh lines.

"Educate me about the Everglades," he demanded, and so there, in the deep shade of the trees, listening to the unceasing chatter of the ever-present starlings, I spoke about the massive wetlands of Florida, the mangrove swamps, gliding alligators and white cranes. He listened intently, as if I were some sort of expert about my state's national treasure.

"I'd like to explore those swamps someday,' he said finally, refusing my help in cleaning up our debris. "I'd love to compare them to the Okavango Delta."

I left him to his task, his sure hands removing every scrap of our lunch, and wandered the fenced confines of the small rest stop. As I watched a cluster of tiny yellow birds dip and swoop around a red-flowered bush, contentment such as I'd never known before stole into my very soul. I glanced back at the trim man busy in his mundane tasks and felt a rush of desire so powerful it nearly took my breath away. Patience, Peter had suggested, so patient I would remain.

We arrived back at Letaba just as the gates closed at 5:30. Peter had paused obediently every time I'd asked to take several more photographs of male impala, and I snapped an especially fine one of a young buck with his head turned toward us, the sun sinking behind him. After parking the jeep, Peter escorted me through the lush camp, pausing as I read each and every one of the markers denoting the various plant species found inside the electric fence. Under his tutelage, I gratifyingly identified more than forty different plants including the lala palm, bushwillow, and umbrella acacia, his quiet manner bolstering my knowledge and confidence. We tarried upon one of the wooden benches overlooking the Letaba River while I fantasized aloud about changing my career and working as a game warden in a place such as this.

I sneaked a glance at Peter. He sat idly gazing over the river, where some sort of antelope had edged down for an evening drink. I suddenly wished I was more like him, so quietly confident and in harmony with his surroundings.

I pensively thought about what Peter had told me about Paul Kruger. Worried about the destruction of the region through rampant hunting and gold prospecting, he had created a preserve to save the flora and the fauna of the area. During our game drive I had discovered that not only was Peter knowledgeable about the park, but passionate about the preservation of its creatures and plants.

He accompanied me to my rondavel that evening after a light supper of warthog stew and salad in the rustic restaurant.

"So, did I pass muster today, ma'am?" he asked lightly.

"It's been the best day of my life," I answered simply.

"So I take it I'm allowed to remain your guide tomorrow?"

"You may accompany me anywhere," I said breathlessly. He had changed from his khakis into dark linen trousers and a short-sleeved white shirt before dinner, and smelled of soap and South African wine.

Peter drew closer and under the moonlight, neither of us aware that a tiny muskrat watched from under a low shrub, he kissed me. It wasn't the sanitized, highly-practiced kiss of Josh the physician, but one from a man of the bush; vibrant, alive, and pulsing with need. He pulled back and stared for a long time into my eyes until finally I gave a small nod. He didn't hesitate as I pulled him into my small but comfortable room. He never faltered as I pulled his shirt from his trousers and struggled with my own clothes. He never complained that the bed was too small or my lips too greedy. I absorbed him like some woman parched from a long drought of love. Peter matched my every kiss and every need, and met tenderness with tenderness. Afterwards, as the moon drenched my bed in lunar caresses, we cuddled in the aftermath of authentic lovemaking. He finally drifted off to sleep, and contentment descended upon me as I lay peacefully in Africa's arms.

I'd never expected that my concept of heaven would turn into a game park, but over the next few days, it did. Peter greeted me each morning with a smile and a kiss before suggesting a route.

I thought nothing could surpass the rustic beauty of Letaba, but after moving to the desert-like Mopani camp and peering at the huge baobab tree that stood smack-center inside the large enclosure, I wasn't sure which I preferred. My small chalet overlooked the brimming dam and that night, having purchased wood to burn in the barbecue, or *braai* pit as the South Africans dubbed it, we listened to the hoarse, mooing cries of the hippo. Peter gave up the pretense of having a separate room and we pushed the two twin beds together in mutual accord.

Peter relayed that Mopani was named after the deciduous mopane tree, which can reach a height of eighteen meters. During July and August its leaves turn yellow, drooping like butterfly wings from which large, leathery pods hang in clusters. I was later to brand the mopane tree the leopard tree, since I continually searched its tall grayish-white trunk in hopes I'd spot one of the large felines draped over its branches. Unfortunately, we never ran into this most elusive of the Big Five. Peter fashioned a chart for me of the flora and fauna of the park to keep careful track of all we encountered. The rhino was our only glimpse of one of the Big Five, and Peter chided me gently about how each and every sighting was a gift when I became impatient. A gift, I reminded myself, just as each and every minute near him was a gift.

Mopani stood high above the Pioneer Dam, its bungalows made of stone and thatch, and my room was more spacious and inviting than my rondavel at Letaba. Each night we piled wood in the braai pit and reviewed the day's sightings. On the way back to camp that first evening, we'd observed a large herd of Burchell's zebra browsing upon dry stalks of grass. They were a marvel with their heavy bellies and plodding ways, bristled tufts of hair standing erect upon their thick, powerful necks. I still half-expected them to exemplify the traditional black-and-white zebras of children's textbooks, but was getting used to this less familiar species.

I felt sure I always missed more animals than I detected, but never once felt let down. Peter made every spotting a joy and an education. His quiet tones instructed me and his gentle arms healed me. Once, we just sat at a nearly-dry waterhole simply to watch the scurrying antics of the common blue-helmeted Guinea fowl. We were content to watch peacefully, munching on sour apples, while countless other cars roared up, shot one exasperated glance at what I was sure they considered folly, and then exited in a cloud of fine dust, Peter's laughter following in their oblivious wake. It was their loss. I could linger for hours, absorbing the sun like the rainbow rock skink I often noted basking upon dusty rocks by the road. Wild Africa and Peter became my lovers, filling the void that had been my own shallow life before this excursion. I never wanted to go home.

"Mandy, quick, get up and grab your camera!" hissed Peter our second evening in Mopani. Startled, I dressed quickly and tiptoed to the door. Peter remained still, dropping a warm arm over my shoulders. Each chalet at Mopani is surrounded by brush and large river boulders, and most overlook the dam. That very afternoon I had rested contentedly upon a large rock and watched a small, rosy lizard bask in the sun.

Now, near that selfsame boulder and illuminated by the flickering reach of flame, an amazing creature crouched, its eyes glowing red in the firelight. Large rounded ears, pointed muzzle, and unique black bars highlighted its burning eyes. The cat-like creature hunched down, warily eyeing us as we stood motionless upon the elevated porch. It had a long-striped, buff-colored feline body spotted with black circles the size of walnuts. It meowed softly. Too large for an African wild cat, the feline possessed a long, slim tail tipped in black. I moved quickly and managed to snap three shots before the creature reacted. The ensuing flash momentarily paralyzed the beautiful, three-foot-long nocturnal predator. The bright glare dissipating, the feline disappeared into the thick shrub without a sound.

Heart thudding, I glanced up at Peter for identification.

"Our nighttime visitor was none other than the large-spotted genet. It's a cat that hides in holes or dense trees by day and turns into the bane of rats and mice at night. She only achieves four pounds or so at maturity. You're lucky to have seen one."

"I am lucky," I whispered and pulled him back into the warmth of our room and pushed-together bed. "So very, very lucky," I repeated as he later smiled above me in the moonlight-drenched chalet.

*It was with some sadness that we departed the dry camp of* Mopani to head for my last camp. We meandered northward with that deep sense of regret accompanying those who know a perfect holiday is nearing an end. Three days remained before I had to catch my return flight to Cape Town, and we planned to make the most of them. Peter assured me he'd contact his sister to book a tour of the wine country and would stay with me at The Vineyard. We made no other plans. There was time for that later.

The northern camp of Shingwedzi seemed relatively old-fashioned when compared with the comfortable newness of Mopani, but nonetheless had its own special charm. It was sufficiently large, with occasional large palm trees mixed with mopanes sporadically dotting the camp. Even now, during the heart of winter, amazing rose and ivory lilies still bloomed. My small two-bed bungalow was comfortable and modern enough. Without a word, our eyes meeting across the bed, we pushed the two twins together. Here, like at Mopani and Letaba, I scribbled down every different tree, animal, and bird I was fortunate enough to spy inside the small notebook Peter had provided for me.

Within all three camps bright glossy starlings, shining metallic blue and possessing strange, orange-red eyes, jumped from branch to branch. Peter took time to identify for me some birds called by the strange name of brubru, and I marveled at the incredible long-tailed shrikes who called out *peeleeo* as they dipped through the thornveld, long wispy tails dangling three full body lengths below them. As always, yellow and red hornbills plagued the camp, sitting haughtily in the trees to glare evilly at us.

My most amazing find was a beautiful little bird called the paradise flycatcher. Its rusty orange tail dangled an extraordinarily two body lengths, and the little fellow sported a bright blue bill. I stalked it for a good fifteen minutes, aiming for the perfect shot, while it eyed me like a model does the camera. Peter lounged on the cement porch, a Castle beer in hand, grinning benevolently at my antics. I stepped up on the porch and sank down beside him.

"Tell me more about your family. I only know about your sister Elizabeth and your crazy skydiving cousin Miles."

He draped his arm over my shoulder in his customary fashion and took a sip of his nearly-warm beer.

"Both my parents are gone now. Dad was a farmer in the north of Zimbabwe. During the 'change of power' our farm was overrun by ex-military cronies under Mugabe. Mum had been a teacher at the local school, and I think it was her history of unrestrained kindness to her students that saved us. Many farmers were killed during that time, but we were spared. The soldiers just sorta 'squatted' on our plot for a couple weeks and then politely came to the door one day and ordered us to go. We were lucky—their guns were pointed downwards. My dad was an ex-missionary who'd always been fair to our workers and Mum—Mum was a saint. So we packed up, my sister nine and me eleven, headed for the bank to withdraw our devaluing money, and slipped across the border into Zambia. We lived there for a while, but Dad never recovered. He had put his heart and soul into that farm, and with it gone, he just couldn't start over."

"I'm so sorry, Peter."

A lovely gray bird with a long, squared-off tail emitted an eerie cry. Peter pointed at it grimly.

"See that bird perched in the mopane tree whose cry resembles the English words 'go away, go away'? The Shona believe that the grey lourie is evil. All I know is that she rested upon our roof the day my father's farm was overrun and ordered us to 'go away, go away.' And so we left Zimbabwe, our home. I've never been much fond of louries since."

In an effort to lighten his dark mood, I asked, "What did your family do in Zambia?"

"Dad worked at the tourist bureau and Mum got a job at the local school. Dad made sure I accompanied him on all our weekend forays into the bush, and taught me everything he knew. Dad maintained such a reverence for life—human or wild—and I was about 14, just before he died, when I decided I desired to be a game guide or park ranger. I traipsed off to South Africa four years later where my cousin Miles had moved and attended Wits, learning everything I could. I acquired a dual degree in Environmental Science and African languages, being fluent in both Shona and Zulu. My sis, Elizabeth, moved first to Namibia, thinking to settle there before transferring down to Stellenbosch. She had a change of heart and obtained her hotel management degree at the university, and married a terrific South African chap."

I gazed past the camp's fence and witnessed a small ferret-like creature dart under the wire mesh. "And your mom?"

"Died several years ago of breast cancer. A real trooper she was, denying anything was remotely wrong with her until the very end. I joined the African Sights Tour Company, leading expeditions into Chobe, the Okavango Delta, and Vic Falls. For another two years I worked in a private reserve that borders

Kruger. Now, I'm freelance and have contracts with several tour agencies that connect to European and North American clients. That's how I was hired by your Ms. Raymond. It's been a grand life and I have no regrets."

"No wife or girlfriends?" I prodded.

He grinned. "Lots of girlfriends, but let's face it, Mandy, most women don't want to compete with the bush."

"How old are you now?"

"Thirty-one. And your mum and family?" he asked gently.

"Just my cousin Ken and Mom now. Ken's folks were killed by a drunk driver, and he lived with us from the age of ten. Dad passed away a few years ago from stomach cancer. My relationship with both my mother and cousin are tenuous at the best. Mom means well, but is controlling and blunt. I always sought to please her and Dad, though nothing I accomplished seemed quite adequate. Ken was always highest on their approval scale. Then I met Josh, and Mom's opinion of me shot *way* up. Thought I'd proven myself by snagging a doctor. Unfortunately, Josh turned out to not be much of a catch. Mom hasn't gotten over the disappointment of my not becoming a doctor's wife."

"Sounds like she and I should have a wee chat," Peter said mildly and gave me a squeeze. "Can't recognize what a gem she's got, I reckon. She *enjoy* critters?"

"No! Mom goes into cardiac arrest if a lizard even comes within ten feet of the house."

Peter tsk-tsked. " I'm positive we'd get on like a house afire."

We conversed little more until much later, after we'd sat down for a simple dinner of chicken and chips and sliced apples. From his always-overflowing ice chest, Peter pulled out my new favorite dessert from South Africa.

"I'd like to go to Crooks' Corner if possible. I hear you can see the shores of Zimbabwe and Botswana from there."

"And just where did you hear that?" asked Peter mildly as he forked out some milk tart.

"Some Australians at Letaba were talking about it. They said they photographed a beautiful buck named the nyala thereabouts."

"You might glimpse one, though the wood's quite dense up near Crooks' Corner. However, we've been very lucky so far. No reason to suspect it won't last. Crooks' Corner it is then." He grinned sexily across the table at me. "So, Miss Mandy, seriously; can you get your sorry bones up before 6:00 a.m. to make a good start?

I sniggered before taking another bite of the delicious tart. "I'm not the one who has trouble getting out of bed, mister!"

# Chapter 8

*Dawn peeked through a faint cover of clouds, the result a* beautiful sunrise, all pink and salmon and luminous. We were listening to the raucous cry of a hornbill when Peter's peripheral vision caught something large, hunched, and spotted. Running parallel to the jeep, the sloping backs of two large spotted hyenas lurched like Quasimodo. At easily one hundred and thirty pounds apiece, they're known to have the strongest jaws of any mammal their size. The bigger one glanced behind him, his large ears protruding nerdishly from a vicious face, and Peter braked the jeep hard as I whipped my camera out, unfortunately catching only a shot of his retreating behind. The other, loping beside his comrade, grinned. His large ears and the orange tuft crowning his head made him resemble some sort of rebellious teenager.

"Another great butt shot," observed Peter before I punched him. We had made a credible start, managing to get out of bed at 5:45 to head for the gate. It was already turning warm. I had noticed the temperature shift after leaving Mopani camp. It was hotter and more humid this far north; consequently I removed my gray sweatshirt and stuffed it into my knapsack, shoving the over-packed bag onto the back seat.

We passed through sandstone hills and mopane plains, Peter noting that while many of the trees were still tinted green this late August, others appeared on the verge of death, the grass surrounding their gray tree trunks brown and short under the wide turquoise bowl of sky stretching overhead. Peter stated it hadn't rained in a good sixteen weeks and the grass had subsequently withered, turning a pale dusty brown.

We crawled at a mere twenty kilometers an hour though the signs permitted fifty, pausing for nearly every bird, bug, and beast. My first real spotting was of a cluster of yellow hornbills picking at a huge pile of dung on the main road. As we paused to watch them, Peter pointed to a large, dark beetle rolling a hefty glob of dung, three times his size, across the road. Occasionally overwhelmed, he twice flipped over the top of the ball. The stalwart dung beetle remained undaunted, keeping to his stinky but apparently necessary mission.

Flies swirled around the huge dung pile. Judging from the clod's giant proportions, it could only have originated from an elephant. The droppings consisted of coarse, undigested bits of twigs and grass, and its freshness filling me with hope that we'd soon run into the large herbivore. As Peter slowly cruised the vacant dirt road, a lovely bird sat perched upon the dead branches of a lightning-struck tree. Its throat was a deep baby-pink; its soft breast resembled a vest of lovely purple encased by turquoise wings. Bright dark eyes and a stately head mistrusted us on sight, and the timid bird flitted away without a sound.

"That's the photogenic lilac-breasted roller, a common subject of nearly every South African nature calendar," said Peter.

"I don't want to buy the calendar. I just want the blasted thing to sit still long enough for a decent shot."

Peter smiled at me lazily, examining me as I angled for the best shot.

"Most women resemble that bird you know."

"Oh?"

Peter sat comfortably in the driver's seat as he scanned the bush. "All pretty-like, but so quick to flit to safety the moment they get a whiff of something remotely unsafe or unfamiliar."

I analyzed him. "Such as you?"

"Well, I'm not exactly considered the greatest catch—living this unstable lifestyle and all."

I lowered my camera and slowly allowed my eyes to savor his lean, tanned face and trim, athletic body. "Stability is much over-rated. And, you don't see me flitting away do you?"

"No. I don't."

My breath caught and I knew that something between us had altered.

"So," he drawled. "Up for more history this early morning, Mandy?"

"Go ahead, professor."

"As you know, over-hunting had nearly wiped out all the big game in the late nineteenth century, so then-president Paul Kruger decided to proclaim the areas between the Sabie and Crocodile Rivers as a game park, dubbing it the Sabie Reserve. After the Anglo-Boer War, two to three thousand indigenous people were forcibly relocated as the park expanded. The last removal of the Makuleke people ended in 1969, allowing Kruger Park to evolve into the world's largest game park. The dispute regarding the rights of the native people and the necessity of preserving habitat for the indigenous creatures still rages today.

It's a never-ending battle, Mandy. I can't make up my mind who's right. Certainly the animals and plants of this region are important, but so are the rights of the misplaced indigenous people. It's a tough call."

"Don't you feel that eco-tourism might be the best and only way to help this country curb South Africa's obvious poverty?" I asked. "Certainly these beautiful birds and animals only benefit from tourists like me."

He smiled. "I'd have to agree. But keeping nature in perfect balance has always got to be the aim. Hey, just there, it's the turnoff for Crooks' Corner."

As we wound through the quiet dirt roads heading north toward Crooks' Corner, I spotted a large female kudu, her broad white stripes helping her blend into the dense woodland. Her majestic mate, his curved horns surely a meter long, chewed on a sprig of grass as he stepped into the open. After a dozen shots we moved slowly onwards again, the wind brushing our faces. Koppie Charaxes butterflies, with thin swallow-tail extensions on their blue-tipped hind wings, danced upon white flowers near the road. In one place where a large, muddy puddle of water seeped gradually onto the road, hundreds of the sunflower-colored butterflies hovered, dipping stylishly into the water before drifting away.

It was with a profound sense of satisfaction that we pulled into Crooks' Corner, situated at the junction of the Limpopo and smaller Luvuvhu River. During the heart of the dry season (the rains wouldn't come again until October), the wide river drifted slowly, only one to two feet high at its deepest point. The roads had remained nearly vacant all morning. We had only passed one game ranger's forest-green vehicle and a small yellow Citi Golf, whose two elderly inhabitants shot us a merry wave.

A musty scent filled the car's interior as the road, hedged in jungle-like trees, opened toward the sandy junction. Birds in the distance alternately cooed, whistled, and warbled, and Peter pointed out the continual hoot of baboons. A leopard tortoise crossed the dirt road slowly; the beautiful pattern upon its yellowish-brown back dubbing it appropriately.

The river stretched wide and far. In the distance, the long neck of a giraffe peeked above the jungle in Mozambique. It was blissfully peaceful and we relaxed with the windows rolled down, contentedly listening to the sounds of the bush and holding hands.

"So here we are, Mandy, at Crooks' Corner. Did you do your homework?"

"I did indeed, sir."

"Alright, young lady, why is it called Crooks' Corner? And no cheating and looking at the information on that stone marker."

"I wouldn't dream of it," I responded, turning my back to the plaque. "This was literally a safe haven for crooks in the 1900s. It didn't matter if you were poacher, gun runner, or killer; the place was safe because you could just dash across the river to avoid the law from the country you were currently in. The coolest thing is that Zimbabwe and Mozambique are just over there."

"Quite right," said Peter, smiling. "It doesn't get the traffic it deserves for being such a famous spot, since it's rather remote. The nearest picnic spot is about ten kilometers away at Pafuri, and you saw how long it took to get here from our own camp. There's an incredible number of birds about. There goes a river warbler. Beautiful, isn't he?"

He was. We both sat contentedly for nearly fifteen minutes, Peter occasionally pointing out a bird species while we listened to the hippos splashing in the river.

Peter finally stirred and gave a lopsided grin. "Well Mandy, I believe nature calls. It's fairly open here, so I should be safe."

I smiled. Peter had marked his territory often during the trip. Sometimes he took his rifle, but today, because of the openness of the clearing, he left it in the rear of the jeep—though his hunter's knife remained securely fastened to his belt. "Back in a few minutes," he said and gave me a sly wink as he tweaked his safari hat at me.

Peter hadn't been gone more than a couple when a white *bakkie*, the South African term for a van, pulled up and an African tourist stepped outside to view the low river. I had scooted over onto the driver's side and was attempting to focus my binoculars upon a large bird foraging in the shallow water. It possessed long yellow legs, a curved yellow bill, and a strange red face. Its body, completely white except for an under-mantle of black feathers, had identified him to Peter as a yellow-billed stork, a fond visitor to large rivers and estuaries.

A sharp rap upon the door startled me. A lanky, tall black man clad in blue jeans and a long-sleeved white shirt grinned impishly at me.

"Excuse me, ma'am. I hope your husband is not in the bush because I see lion tracks just there. He should not have gotten out of the car."

I must have appeared startled. "Husband?" I felt quite flattered at Peter being identified as my spouse. I shifted in my seat, ready to call out and warn Peter. "Do you really think there's danger?"

The concerned visitor laughed sharply and suddenly lunged, grabbing my hair and twisting back my head. "But of course. It's dangerous to travel these roads alone, Mama."

The jeep was suddenly surrounded by four black men, two holding handguns. At just that moment I realized every woman's nightmare: I was going to be raped and robbed. My captor jerked open the dusty jeep's door and dragged me from the vehicle by my hair, twisting my arm viciously behind me. I cried out in pain while his accomplices scanned the wide parking area and neighboring bush. Only one road led to Crooks' Corner. Traffic in this remote corner was sparse at best, and these men knew it.

"Get into the back!" the thin man barked. He flung open the door and threw me into the backseat of the jeep before scurrying to the driver's seat. A stocky, short man with dreadlocks lowered himself into the passenger seat while a heavyset man with small, cold eyes and spiked tufts of hair joined me in the back. My arm and hair ached from their abuse. The fat man next to me, resembling a shorn porcupine, reeked of body odor and waved a pistol in front of my dazed eyes.

Peter! Where was Peter? I frantically scanned the dense scrub surrounding the large turn-around area. The gaunt man gunned the engine and tore out of the huge, circular lookout point, followed by the dusty white van. I strived to memorize the license plate, straining at the effort of focusing on the bobbing rectangle in the ensuing cloud of dust. HCJ 805 NW.

My captors spoke loudly in their own native tongue, the argument intense as I curled myself as far away from my smelly seatmate as I could. The emaciated hijacker drove wildly, suddenly veering off the main dirt road to crash through the brush. Only a few minutes later, the kidnapper made another abrupt turn south. I remembered from the map and Peter's tutelage that this was wild country with no real public access. The driver remained tense as heated arguments in their native language flew around me. I dreaded to learn what topic they debated. I glanced out of the rearview mirror to note the bakkie still followed, dust and rocks flying behind its balding tires. For just an instant, I swore I glimpsed Peter running parallel to the river. It was a fruitless, pathetic hope. He couldn't have been there.

The hijacker drove wildly for twenty minutes, dodging thorn trees, scattering small, brown coveys of speckled birds, and once disturbing a long-haired antelope resembling the kudu I had seen earlier. My numb mind recognized it as the elusive nyala. My backpack had fallen onto the backseat floor and the modishly-dreadlocked African fiddled greedily with my new camera and binoculars. He couldn't know that Peter's rifle was stowed in the back under a blanket. If I could somehow just reach back there! I had never used a gun in my life, but it had to be simple, didn't it? My heavy seatmate turned pebble black-eyes on me and lasciviously examined my body. I instinctively knew without a shadow of a doubt that if I didn't get out of this jeep soon, I was going to be assaulted and probably murdered. Later, I'd be tossed from the vehicle without a shred of conscience, to become food for the scavengers.

We traveled full throttle, holding parallel to the Limpopo River where huge logs, rocks, and debris littered its wide banks. The road became increasing rough as the jeep crashed by the dusty scenery. A crazy plan struck me. If I could somehow manage to leap from the 4x4, the jeep probably couldn't follow me down the embankment. My kidnappers still adhered to a rough track that had probably once served as a maintenance road. If I planned to bolt, it was now or never. They hit a particularly large bump and the driver cursed in his own language while my seatmate clutched the headrest in front of him. I leaned over and grabbing my bulging backpack, jerked at the stiff door handle and plunged headfirst into the road as the dust billowed around me.

It was probably that choking dust which saved me, since the bakkie had dropped ten or so yards back, its driver straining to achieve more visibility as he steered through the blinding cloud. My shoulder hit the ground hard and though badly bruised and shaken, I leaped to my feet and tore past the rear of the jeep, sprinting for the wide shores of the Limpopo River. I crashed through the dense underbrush as the screech of brakes, followed by men shouting hoarsely, echoed above the harsh din of the car motors. I paid them no heed, desperately plunging down the embankment toward the river, swerving between dirty white boulders and protruding tree trunks in my frenzied effort to escape.

The telltale zing and ricochet of a bullet whizzed by my head, and I realized their intent. I must be killed quickly to avoid an eyewitness to their crime. Two of the men tore off after me and I suddenly had cause to bless the aerobics classes I faithfully attended four times a week as I careened pell-mell through the veldt. Another bullet whizzed past my cheek and a third kicked up the dust in front of me. Amazingly, the searching bullets missed me entirely, though the befuddled men fired at least half a dozen rounds. Even in my desperate attempt at escape, my heart and head cried out for Peter. If only I could get to him. Another bullet whizzed past my head and actually cropped some of my hair.

I could sense rather than see one of the men gaining on me, the thud of his feet echoing against the dusty earth. I swerved into a thorn bush, which tore at my cheek and ripped my long-sleeved t-shirt. Another burst of fire issued from the embankment and a cry of agony erupted from somewhere behind me. They had shot one of their own! It didn't slow me down one iota. As I reached the vast expanse of the river, the notion that crocodiles, snakes, or even a lion might be near never occurred to me. I simply plunged noisily into the water, oblivious to any other danger than the pursuing men. The river spanned a hundred feet wide and at one point I nearly went down; the water suddenly swirling just below my hips, and deeper than I expected. I didn't falter, the fear of death propelling me toward the seeming safety of Mozambique. Wild shouting reverberated behind me and I could discern some of their desperate words.

"You must come back, ma'am! You will die in the *bundu,* for the lions will eat you! We won't hurt you, Mama! Come back!"

It was a no-brainer. I'd rather risk being eaten by lions than being raped and murdered by ruthless hijackers. I ran until I could run no more, finally dropping heavily by a sycamore fig tree in a desperate attempt to catch my breath. I roused within a few seconds, some sense of preservation propelling me up into the huge tree. The fig's roughly gnarled trunk provided a nearly horizontal overhang, which I scampered up onto like a frightened monkey. There, with chest heaving and backpack perched by my side, I rested and watched.

Minutes ticked by, but no one pursued. Only the trill of some bird in the bush and the distant gurgle of water disturbed the midday calm. Finally it struck me why I heard nothing. They simply hadn't followed me any farther. Their common sense indicated that as a woman alone in the wilds, a citified tourist with no survival skills, they didn't need to find me. They had assumed, quite correctly, that the bush would prove my eventual graveyard. Given time, my body would be torn apart by greedy scavengers, my corpse a mute witness to their crimes. They didn't believe that I had ever been accompanied by a man. They'd never seen Peter in the jeep, and because I sat in the driver's seat, assumed I was alone. I shivered forlornly, only now realizing my folly. They were indeed correct. I had only seemingly escaped. In actuality, I was completely and utterly alone, totally lost in the bush and with Peter nowhere to be found.

# Chapter 9

*Thirty minutes later, after uselessly alternating between* tears and rage, I pulled myself together enough to rummage through my backpack. I removed my gray sweatshirt and laid the bag's paltry contents upon it. My treasure trove consisted of four energy bars, a box of Lion matches, one penlight flashlight with extra batteries, two small tissue packs, an open pack of cherry gum, dental floss, a nearly full two-liter bottle of spring water, antacid tablets, an extra hair tie, a small pack of *biltong* (the South African version of jerky), two large bags of salted peanuts, three apples, a pen, my small notepad and, God be praised, my Swiss army knife.

This was all that separated me between life and death in the African bush. I fingered the items glumly. Why hadn't I packed more food and water for God's sake? My map, binoculars, camera, and guidebook had rested near the console of the jeep and my wallet, chalet key, and park pass were in the vehicle's dash. A loud *tink-tink* sound caused me to jerk and the gum, floss, and bottled water bounced into the dark foliage below.

It was only a pair of noisy black and white plovers aggressively warning away a large, cream egret-type bird, and I laughed shakily. Replacing all my gear inside the small backpack and swinging it over my sweaty shoulders, I cautiously half-slid, half-crept down the huge tree. I collected the fallen items scattered about and brushed off several oversized black ants now crawling over them. Sweeping the items back into my carryall, I crept back up the tree again to sit perched like some misshapen cat upon the sycamore fig's wide branches.

Of course I'd forgotten that this was the very type of tree that leopards or deadly snakes might prefer. For now, its shady branches simply offered a safe haven, a refuge while I tried to collect my wits and decide what to do next. My cheek felt damp and I touched it tentatively, my finger coming away red from a jagged tear inflicted by the thorn tree. I removed one of the tissues and dabbed absently, wishing with all my heart that I had a better sense of direction. Peter had spoken about the Pafuri rest stop some ten kilometers distant; maybe he'd recall the comment and head that way. I stifled a sob. Peter would find me. He had to. He was an expert in the bush. Maybe if I just waited, he'd stumble upon me. So I delayed for nearly an hour.

Finally, the need to relieve myself forced me from my awkward perch. I hung my bag on a nearby branch and, grabbing one of the small tissues, crept down the gray, mottled trunk. Bright orange dragonflies flitted near the bank. In a false sense of modesty, I crouched in the bushes while glancing around jerkily. I had just finished when something ran past my trainers. I leaped up, letting out a sharp squeak. A small, yellow-tinged ground squirrel scurried through the bush. Jeez, one tiny little rodent and I was nearly plunged into cardiac arrest!

Disgusted, I pocketed the remaining tissues and returned to the upper branches, realizing I needed to formulate a plan. Help was foremost. If I could get back to the road, a car would certainly pass by. I'd alert the compassionate inhabitants that my companion was missing and they'd return me to Crooks' Corner, where Peter likely waited.

My stomach growled and I contemplated eating one of the energy bars and apples. Well, why not? If I was lucky I'd find the main road and flag down a passing vehicle within an hour or so; therefore, after little deliberation, I gave myself permission to eat. After devouring the bar and tossing the core onto the ant-laden ground, still hungry, I demolished half of the first bag of peanuts as well, washing them down with a huge swig of water.

Feeling immensely better, I took time to mourn the fact that I hadn't managed to somehow retain the map. How was I supposed to find Peter or Crooks' Corner without one? I closed my eyes and sought to visualize the direction in which I'd traveled.

Crooks' Corner is located as far northeast as the road will go. To get there we'd wound through the thick tropical forest upon the eastern road overlooking the Luvuvhu River before turning north. Crooks' Corner stands only three kilometers off the road. After a few moments of contemplation I realized that all I really needed to do was stay on this side of the Limpopo River and head north. I figured we'd driven perhaps fifteen minutes on the service road and I'd run at least twenty. If I followed the river, I estimated that within two hours I'd reach the wide, circular lookout point designating Crooks' Corner. I bowed my head and sent up a small prayer, asking my Maker to guide me to Peter and safety.

I slipped down the tree once again and, removing the Swiss army knife, slipped it into my pocket. It's amazing what a false sense of security the small red knife provided me. As an afterthought, I picked up a fist-sized stone in my right hand, ready to fling it at any beast who dared approach. I had a momentary vision of myself, a yellow-eyed lion slinking ever closer as I let loose a lethal stone, bouncing it squarely off her nose. The poor, bloodied beast would deliver one pained, catlike whimper and bound off, never to be heard of again. I grinned to myself. Everyone must be allowed Walter Mitty dreams, even a coward like me.

With the sound of the sluggish river gurgling on my left and the warmth of the sun upon my shoulders, it was probably a beautiful day. Unfortunately, I felt too anxious and desperate to appreciate anything but my need to find the road and Peter. The only wildlife seemed to be a countless array of birds I could not name or number. I plodded on for nearly forty minutes, my confidence rising. Finally, needing a breather, I lowered my aching body down upon a log and examined the embankment paralleling the river. The Limpopo is a leisurely watercourse, meandering half-heartedly through the brush and flood pan. However, I knew from my reading that its gentle appearance can be deceiving. During February 2000, pounding summer rains drenched Southern Africa and swelled the river to monstrous levels, flooding vast areas of Mozambique and killing thousands.

It felt good to rest, and I spent a few minutes observing a bright, double-winged flying insect hovering near me. A low, moaning grunt from behind caused me to jump in alarm from my makeshift bench. The crocodile was enormous, measuring at least eight feet long. He rested, his long, yellowish tail half-submerged in the water, and eyed me, those gleaming orbs atop his head unblinking and unfeeling. Thank God, the log was positioned between him and me! With a start I realized he wasn't the only

Nile crocodile present; at least half a dozen others basked upon the wet sand. How careless I'd been. This was crocodile territory. Hadn't Peter told me how they routinely killed scores of Africans each year?

I edged slowly away from the reptile-infested river, facing a dilemma. Dare I continue following the shoreline, or should I climb the embankment in an effort to distance myself from the hungry crocs? But, I argued with myself, who knew what even more foul forms of wildlife lurked in the dense underbrush? The ancient reptile took an elevated step toward me, perched upon short bowed legs. His steady advance decided me. I scrambled up the steep bank, the shrubs tearing at my jeans and backpack. A narrow animal trail opened to my right, grass beaten down by countless creatures' pilgrimages to the water. This seemed the likely choice. It would prove a fair sight easier going than tromping through the high grass. I was hopeful the trail would remain parallel to the river.

I followed the narrow ribbon of trail for a quarter of a mile, scanning the dense brush continually for both predators and Peter, until I tripped and banged my knees. It just wasn't possible to watch the bush and the path at the same time. Staggering to my feet, I set off again, pausing once to rub my aching kneecaps.

I was almost as surprised as they when I stumbled upon a pair of waterbuck whose long, gray, shaggy coats covered sturdy bodies emblazoned with the telltale white rings upon their bottoms. The couple whirled, allowing me a wonderful view of their toilet-seat rears as they bounded through the foliage. At least these creatures were harmless. I concentrated on moving more cautiously and quietly, realizing I'd been lucky so far. Unfortunately, my lack of stealth made it impossible for me to move silently, no matter how hard I tried. After another five minutes, the well-worn trail veered inland and away from the river, to which I knew I had to keep if I were to ever find my way back to Crooks' Corner and Peter. I paused by large, grayish-white boulders jetting out over the river, hedged by shiny-leafed shrubs.

I glanced at my watch. It was almost half past two. In winter, darkness completely cloaks Southern Africa by six in the evening. If I continued following the animal track, I would move further back into Mozambique, so my only choice was to cross the river and return to the South African side of Kruger. I hesitated, not wishing to venture anywhere near where the hijackers had waylaid me. Perhaps there were roads on the Mozambican side. No, I chided myself. Kruger had countless tourists traveling its well-maintained roads. My best chance lay within its boundaries, not in the less-managed wilds of Mozambique.

I cautiously ventured down onto the sandbank again, a pair of hammer-headed birds scurrying away at my approach. I strained my neck searching for crocs, though none lay lazily upon nearby sandbars. I stood for a moment and pondered. Should I leisurely pick my way across the wide, shallow river, or simply tear across in hopes of thwarting any attack by crocodiles or other predators? I inhaled deeply, readjusted my pack, and chose the latter.

The river, only knee-height, dampened my dirty jeans as I raced across its wide gulf. I stumbled once, my feet dragging in the wet sand. A snowy bird flapped angrily as it rose above the shallow water, but I ignored her, sprinting until dry soil crunched beneath my feet. Scrambling up the bank, I paused atop a boulder to catch my breath. Unfortunately, this side looked identical to the other. It was imperative that I find the sandy track the hijackers had used. As I descended the boulder, I decided that if I heard the approach of any vehicle, I'd duck behind a shrub until I determined whether the drivers were friend or foe.

Crossing my fingers, I headed directly west and stumbled upon the road within three minutes. A miracle! Now, if I just followed the track, where recent tire impressions clearly disturbed the dry sand, I should make it to Crooks' Corner within an hour. My heart swelled and feeling almost gleeful, I managed a short fantasy about Peter, envisioning myself encircled by enthralled park rangers as he proudly lifted his sandy head, his dusky eyes filled with joy, while I recounted my thrilling tale of escape and survival.

It hit me suddenly that I wanted Peter to believe me competent and intelligent. That daydream moved me into action. Halting abruptly, I removed my small notebook and wrote down the bakkie's license plate number before I forgot it. HCJ 805 NW. I also scribbled a brief description of the white van with its banged-up rear fender, as well as a clear description of my captors. I went on to describe my dusty, rented jeep and everything that had been left inside it. Unfortunately, I had less luck remembering the rental's license plate number than that of my kidnappers.

I shoved the small notepad back into my backpack and took a long drink of water before setting off at a brisk jog. Breathless within ten minutes, I slowed down, deciding a swift walk wouldn't tax my endurance as much as a run. As long as I made it to the main road within the hour, I would be just fine.

A strange, rasping sound startled me from my thoughts and I swung my eyes upward. Rearing up before me, not more than two yards distant, its long, charcoal body stretching across the entire expanse of the sandy track, loomed every hiker's nightmare. The snake lifted a coffin-shaped head, its curved mouth fixed in an odd perpetual smile. I screamed as the serpent turned, rearing at least four feet in the air, its open mouth, black as night, hissing in warning. The only identification I could make through my panic was this was definitely not a cobra and must measure at least ten feet long.

I screeched and plunged off the dirt road, certain I heard the swish of the snake's heavy body pursuing me into the brush. The rasping noise of its scales scraped the dirt directly behind me and I shrieked again. A large troop of baboons hooted and scattered into the trees as I tore past, too preoccupied to do little more than note their presence. I ran for what seemed ages, the rough scraping noise of the massive serpent's scales indicating it remained right at my heels, intent on biting me at all costs.

Now, how could any snake be that fast and that persistent, a more rational mind might have wondered? But where snakes were concerned, I didn't possess a single cogent bone in my body. I ran for at least a mile before a strange sort of mocking awareness crept over me. If I slowed (as I was rapidly tiring), the swishing noise slowed; if I speeded up, it speeded up too, sounding so close the serpent had to be practically upon me. I halted suddenly and the rasping noise of the snake's scales ceased entirely. I stumbled a few paces in bewilderment before realizing dumbly that the pursuing noise I'd identified as belonging to the smiling snake as it surged against the ground was nothing more than my denim-clad legs rubbing against each other. Mortified, I paused by a thorny tree and cursed heartily, having proven beyond a shadow of a doubt what a citified fool I was! Thank God Peter hadn't seen my frenzied retreat. The thought of what he'd think forced tears into my eyes.

The sweat poured off my face, and my back felt bruised from the pack's violent banging against my spine. Humiliation nearly overwhelmed me, but it took quite a while for an even worse fact to sink in. In my frantic plunge through the dense undergrowth of the veldt, I'd lost the road entirely. Again disoriented, I spent the next hour frantically searching for the rough track the hijackers had used to steal the jeep. Though I tried to retrace my steps east toward the river, I couldn't, for the life of me, relocate the wide Limpopo. The thieves' tire imprints had been fresh in the dry sand and I consoled myself with the fact that since I'd found them once, I could surely do so again. But, as the minutes ticked rapidly toward sundown, my terror increased. I wandered half-dazed through the bush until finally, sweating and fatigued, I sank down upon a flaky stump, acknowledging for the first time that I was thoroughly and completely lost; an American idiot in paradise with my savior lover nowhere to be found.

# Chapter 10

---

*At now nearly 4:00 p.m., I realized that if I didn't find the main* road and Peter soon I'd lack shelter and warmth for the night. I had only ninety minutes until the gates closed at five thirty and probably thirty minutes of light left after that. While I might be lucky enough to run into some tourists doing a night drive, chances were slim. Instinct insisted that the Limpopo River had to be close, but in what direction? A lovely slim lizard with a long, electric-blue tail and striped body wiggled out into the ground before me. Clearly harmless, he now seemed my only friend, and so I directed the question at him.

"So which way do you think I should go, little guy?" I asked as the lizard basked in the bright sun. The reptile twitched its vivid blue tail and, considering that as much of a sign as anything else, I re-shouldered my backpack and began trudging in the direction his tail pointed.

A light cloud cover darkened the sky. While threatening no rain, it did succeed in confusing me as to the sun's true direction. I walked slowly, hoping I was headed east. The late afternoon grew chilly and my stomach ached from tension. Worse yet, I seemed to be having an allergic reaction because my skin itched and crawled underneath my damp clothing. An unseen root caught at my trainer and I plunged facedown into the dirt, eating sand. Spitting and coughing, I dragged myself into a shallow indentation in the soil not far from some acacia trees.

Like a hopeless child I burst into tears, the salt stinging my torn cheek. Despair visited me that hour just before dusk as I lay trembling, curled into a tight ball in a fruitless effort to try to retain my waning body heat. Black ants scurried near my face and the evening sounds escalated, adding to my ripening fear.

It was then I spotted her. Her eyes glowed yellow in the dimming light as her elfish ears tilted toward me. She remained frozen in mid-stride as she analyzed how viable a meal I'd make. How had it come to this?

The cat's yellow eyes bored into my hazel ones. Never a champion at staring contests, something broke inside me. Whether it was fear, despair about Peter and my situation, stupidity, or some belated sense of courage that propelled me, I'll never know.

I suddenly lurched to my feet, screaming and roaring, clapping my hands together like some frenzied exercise nut performing clownish jumping jacks. The feline's eyes flamed and she leaped—not at me but away, springing gracefully over low bushes and grass. Madness overtook my senses and I chased her, screaming like a wild banshee. I remained as sure-footed and almost as swift as she. The caracal suddenly leaped, springing in a graceful arch that landed her upon the sandy shores of the river.

I stopped like some sort of demented lemming halted at the edge of the cliff it had nearly plunged over. Standing gratefully upon the rocky embankment, I stared once again at the wide

Limpopo. The frightened cat had led me to its sluggishly moving waters. I sank down upon my bottom and gazed at its banks, cherishing its wide, languid shores like a lost lover regained. The distant grunting of submerged hippos echoing through the riverbank stirred up a belated sense of reason in my fatigued brain. With little chance of finding the main road before dark, I had to face the fact that I was stuck in the bush for the night. I tried to remember all the tidbits of information Peter had shared about his walking safaris. I recalled how he and his clients had slept atop their jeeps in a portable tent—hoisted away from lions, snakes, and other harmful creatures.

Scanning the curving banks of the river, I searched for an elevated place to shelter. Perhaps one of those huge fig trees I'd climbed after escaping the hijackers would do. In its protective branches I could craft a nest for the night. After a cautious quarter of a mile, I stumbled upon the perfect tree. Nestled within a clump of three similar trees with huge, buttressed trunks and powdery yellowish-orange bark, my chosen refuge hung over the sandy embankment, presenting an uninterrupted view of the meandering river. Behind it, a semi-clearing seemed ideal for building a fire. After climbing the huge trunk, I discovered a broken branch perfect for hanging my backpack safely away from baboons and other creatures.

I shimmied down and, now shivering, began foraging for dry wood in the dim light. Luckily, driftwood plentifully dotted the sandy expanse of the Limpopo River. I pulled several large pieces out of the sand and dragged them toward my little clearing. Perfect. Unfortunately, without kindling I'd have no way to ignite the large pieces. Twenty yards away, a broken log, bent branches extending like a pincushion from its decaying trunk, rose from the sandy soil. I hastily twisted small twigs off its reluctant surface until a sharp sting upon my knuckle halted me. A bright red ant, the length of my fingernail, crawled across the back of my hand. Fire ants scurried everywhere and with a sharp cry I dropped the branch and frantically beat off the swarm. I stood right in their nest! Hopping back, I still felt the hot sting of a renegade soldier's attack beneath my trouser leg. Beating frantically at my already bruised leg, I stumbled away.

A few yards away, some dry-looking twigs peeked from under a crumbling rock. Straining with the effort, I pulled mightily, finally toppling the small boulder. A black scorpion, tail curved menacingly over its shiny body, scuttled toward my foot. Shrieking loudly, I leaped over the boulder and the arachnid darted into the deep shadow of a river rock. After that, incredibly tentative and literally jumping at every shadow, it took me a full fifteen minutes just to gather enough twigs to start a fire.

Like a conscientious Girl Scout, I carefully positioned saucer-sized stones in an attempt to encircle the fire pit as a preventive measure, hoping to contain any sparks that might start the dry grass ablaze. Thank goodness I had my box of matches. I decided to wait until it was almost completely dark to light my fire. I now had enough wood to last several hours; hopefully, that would keep away any predators.

Hunger gnawed at my innards as I considered my limited meal choices. I could finish off the peanuts, eat another energy bar, have one of the apples, or tuck into the biltong. Any of those options would leave little for breakfast or lunch. After consuming a long drink of water I decided to search for something edible from the veldt to make my meager supplies last longer. Late-blooming flowers lined the riverbank, resembling tall, red-blossomed matchsticks. At nearly a meter high, small clusters of peanut-sized red berries clung to their bottom stems. I'd been lectured all through my growing years by my farm-bred grandmother about how one must be extremely cautious regarding what they consume from nature. Her own cousin had died a horrible death from ingesting poisonous toadstools.

But how was I to determine if the berries were poisonous or not? I finally decided that dinner this night would simply have to consist of an energy bar, a few peanuts, one apple, and some bottled water. I momentarily wondered if there were any fish in the shallow Limpopo, but after recalling my experience with the crocodile, decided that finding out might not be such a wise idea.

A snort and a crackle issued from the brush and I immediately scrambled up the fig tree, perched upon the overhanging branch with my feet drawn up, ready to crawl higher if the need arose. A very large grayish-brown baboon came out of the bush and sniffed about, his weight resting on his knuckles. He scanned the riverbank before emitting a low howl, apparently beckoning his troop. Realizing that trees are a second home to baboons, I crouched silently, alert to the intruder's every move. Peter had warned me about the aggressive Chacma baboons with their large canines and troops numbering up to a hundred. I had hoped since Letaba to see one close-up on my journey. One should be careful what one wishes for.

The first baboon to emerge from the bush was a huge male, his dusty fur bristling. He sat on his haunches and manipulated his large testicles. The sight was unnerving. A smaller male baboon smacked the back of his head like a teacher does an offending student, and the leader and several others of his troop chased after him, dashing across the sandy bank. The others of the group, apparently thirsty, leaned down with their lips close to the water and drank noisily. A few stragglers, mostly young mothers with children balanced upon their backs and leaning against their upright tails, began foraging the same tall flowers I'd analyzed earlier. I watched in keen interest as they peeled off the berries and popped them into their mouths, chewing just like humans. I smiled to myself; here was a surefire method to determine if the berries were edible or not. Hopefully the baboons would leave me enough to snack upon later.

Luckily the baboons did not linger long. The females soon quit their foraging and sauntered down to the river for drinks before heading north. The troop followed the bank, keeping away from the water to instinctively avoid lurking crocodiles. However, they took their own sweet time about it and a full fifteen minutes passed before the last baboon disappeared from sight.

By now, nearly paralyzed from perching on the scaly branch, I slid down the first few feet and then jumped, leaping upon the soft sand beneath the tree. Numb from lack of circulation, I landed first upon my stinging feet before falling straight upon my bottom, my rubbery legs failing to support me. I spent the next few minutes rubbing them briskly and noting how cool it suddenly had become. The sun obstinately faded behind the opposite stand of trees and I realized I needed to immediately start my fire after foraging for the last bit of berries while there was still enough light to see.

The baboons hadn't left much. After picking through all the flowery bushes I found only two scant handfuls. My next dilemma was whether to eat them immediately or go wash them in the river. I decided that if they hadn't killed the baboons then they probably wouldn't harm me, so I popped one of the berries into my mouth. Though tart and mushy, I managed to swallow it down. By sheer effort of will I finished eating all the berries, thankful that at least they stopped my stomach rumbling. I decided to eat only half an energy bar and one of the tart apples, saving the rest of my hoard for tomorrow.

After retrieving matches from the backpack, I arranged the dry kindling and lit the first match. I don't know why I thought it was going to be easy to light the dry twigs. Shouldn't one of the small matches strike the tinder, instantly bursting it into flame? How wrong I was. After four worthless strikes I realized that if I wasn't careful I'd not only lack a fire, but would soon be out of matches. Certainly Indiana Jones and Lara Croft had never dealt with this type of problem!

I'd been a Girl Scout, but to observe me fumbling about, one would have been convinced I'd flunked out of the organization. The kindling smoked, but refused to ignite. The dirty branches, some of which had thorns that tore at my hands, kept falling out of my precise cone-shaped stack. While my mishaps would have been a hit on *America's Funniest Home Videos,* it was no laughing matter to me. I once again imagined my competent Peter quickly lighting a fire and smiling indulgently at my clumsiness. The temperature continued to drop and I paused to pull my dark-gray sweatshirt over my long-sleeved tee and rub my cold hands upon my filthy jeans. The days might be pleasant and warm during August in South Africa, but the evenings turned uncomfortably cold.

I refused to give up. I not only needed a fire for warmth, but protection as well. How many countless wildlife shows and thrilling books had convinced me that animals were instinctively afraid of fire? I also housed the vague hope that my feeble flames would serve as a beacon either to Peter, if he was still alive, or to game wardens eager to investigate an illegal campfire, who would thus discover me. Peter, still alive—the image of his warm steady eyes and loving smile strengthened me. So I knelt and huffed and puffed, just like the wolf in the story of the three little pigs, until finally my fifth match took. I can state with unfaltering certainty that fire is a miracle. I'm now convinced that it is the ability to make fire, as well as flush toilets, which really separates man from beast. More devout than I'd ever been before, I sent up a swift, thankful prayer to my Maker while gradually adding small twigs and larger branches until I achieved a roaring blaze. I then moved a fairly flat stump near the fire and basked in its warmth.

Later, as I munched on some salty peanuts and dry biltong, (the tart berries in no way could sustain me) I gazed fretfully into the dancing fire, remembering a program on *Animal Planet* about how mountain gorillas and orangutans make nests to sleep in every night. The idea of a soft nest sounded cozy, but was it feasible? Perhaps I should sleep in the tree, which would be much safer, instead of a comfy bed near the fire. Indecisively I gazed at the fire, reluctant to move away from its cheerful flames.

Exhausted, hungry and dispirited, I pondered how all this could have happened to me. My life had always been tightly controlled and well-organized. I felt as shell-shocked and befuddled as when I'd discovered Josh's unfaithfulness.

I forced myself to redirect my thoughts as panic shot through me. I had to focus on the current problems at hand. The descending chill made me hesitant to exchange the warmth of the fire and my cozy stump for the tree. I argued with myself that if I stretched out by the well-tended fire, fell asleep and let it go out, there was a strong possibility I would wake up face-to-face with a leopard. I weighed my options for several minutes and finally decided the fire was the best choice. Better to be warm and flat than fall from a cold tree and break my back. Resolutely, I collected a pile of leaves and grass for my itchy bed, careful to avoid ones with thorns or the ever-present ants.

I gathered a few more sticks of wood using my penlight as a guide, praying I'd collected enough to maintain the fire all night. I opened up another one of my energy bars and ate it slowly, savoring every bite before devouring another tart green apple and more peanuts. The cold made me ravenous and now only a scant fistful of nuts, a tidbit of biltong, one energy bar, and the last apple remained for breakfast. I had only shoved one two-liter water bottle into my backpack, and scarcely a quarter of it remained. The river gurgled in the distance, and I decided it was time for me to venture down to the river and refill the bottle. Hopefully the water wasn't polluted or filled with those horrible parasites I'd heard infested the waterways of Africa. I gulped down the remaining water and searched for a weapon.

While I had been clearing the brush from near my fire, I'd discovered a fairly long staff. Using my Swiss army knife I removed the remaining thorns and protrusions, leaving myself a heavy-duty, formidable weapon. Best yet, tomorrow it could also serve as a walking stick. Using the penlight as a guide I retraced the path the baboons had taken. I'd watched them stoop to drink in a little side pool off the main waterway, and I headed for that. Upon inspection, the water appeared fairly clean in the narrow beam of my small flashlight. The hum of night insects filled the air as I dunked my water bottle into the stream, filling it to the brim before kneeling down for a long drink.

A slight rustle sounded to my left and never pausing to ascertain its identity, I grabbed up my water bottle and staff and bolted for the safety of the fire. From where I'd knelt to drink, I'd noticed that my fire sent up a swirl of smoke and sparks from its bed of bright, flaming wood and coals. I hoped the blaze would serve as a proper SOS for Peter or anyone else searching for me. I had no more reached my fire and sank down on my makeshift seat when the night dropped like a heavy black curtain. I shivered, more from fear than cold, and fed the fire two more unnecessary logs.

The wind picked up, chilling me further. It seemed no matter where I moved, the smoke followed and I spent most of my time dragging my stump to new positions to escape the choking fumes. Some of the wood was clearly wet, little bubbles of sap oozing from the ends of the smoking sticks. One log I placed upon the dismal fire stank, its reek so pungent that I grabbed up my fire poker and hurtled the offending log to the ground, burying it in the sand.

Gradually, the wind died down and the fire eased its smoking torment. I moved closer, thinking what a wonderful night this would be if I wasn't so frightened. Jerking and convulsing at every little noise, I barely noticed the brilliant Milky Way, so vivid it appeared close enough to touch. Crickets hummed about me and in the distance, I heard the hoot of hunting owls. Occasionally, the night bird's short, concise hoots were joined by the noisy baboons' deeper bellows. I sat feeding my fire, flinching at every new sound and debating whether or not to stretch out upon my nest.

The inevitable finally arrived; bedtime had come. Grabbing one of my valuable tissues, I obeyed the call of nature. I washed my hands in the sand like the ancient Arabs and settled down upon my rough bed. It took a long time to fall asleep; my memories of how just last night Peter had held me, breathing sleepily into my hair, awakened my tears again. I ached as much inside as out. The fear, discomfort and homesickness for Peter made me an insomniac even though I lay exhausted. Finally the distant murmur of the river and comforting rustle of the breeze did their magic. With my staff clutched to my chest, the army knife by my cheek, and the trusty penlight within reach, I drifted into a dreamless sleep.

# Chapter 11

---

*I awoke with a start. Only coals remained from my fire, so* I could make out only the faint outline of something nosing around my foot. Willing myself not to scream, I furiously kicked at the moving object, my staff held ready to defend myself from whatever the assailant might be. Leaping to my feet, I noted a scaly round ball just outside my fire pit and soundly clubbed the bowling-ball-sized shape like one would a golf ball. It rolled to the outer edge of the brush I had cleared earlier that evening. Quickly stacking a few dry logs onto the fire, I blew on the coals and the dry wood immediately burst into bright flame to brilliantly illuminate the area.

To my amazement, the ball slowly unfurled, transforming into a bizarre creature. An upper body covered with horny scales was no less unique than its long, narrow snout which resembled that of an anteater or armadillo. I later ascertained that this reptilian-looking creature was none other than the nocturnal pangolin. Hindsight proved that it was a harmless animal that fed only on termites and ants, but at the time I could only note its sharply curved black claws. After unrolling from its tight ball, the pangolin turned a head quizzically toward me before stumbling off into the underbrush. I laughed shakily, realizing it had simply been on a search for termite mounds.

Glancing at my wristwatch, I noted it was now quarter after midnight; I had slept for almost four hours. I fed more logs onto the fire and sat for a long time listening to the night sounds of the untamed bush. It was then that I heard it; a low, guttural bellow in the distance, sounding in monotonous repetition. Even I, a rank amateur lost in the bush, recognized the call of the lion. Echoing more than a mile away, its repetitive low roars indicated to me it sought others of its kind. That realization drove my blood pressure up as I visualized a hungry pride encircling my small campsite, licking their collective chops as they spotted a suitable midnight snack.

I slept little the rest of that night and when I finally awoke a few minutes after dawn, my stiff muscles were thoroughly chilled. The fire had burned out; even its coals no longer were glowing, but I'd survived the night. I allotted myself the rest of the biltong for breakfast, determined I would snack on the last of the peanuts, remaining apple and energy bar later. I wolfed down the strong, gamey jerky; the dried meat had become flushed a murky crimson. While appearing undercooked and unappetizing, to me it was the tastiest breakfast in the world. I then wandered over to see if there were any more berries I might have missed from where the baboons had foraged the previous night, but no such luck. After a swig of tepid water, I kicked sand over the dead coals and repacked my bag.

Last night, as I'd lain awake trembling at the distant roar of the lion, I'd made a tentative plan. I would follow the river until I hit the road or Crooks' Corner: whichever came first. Then I'd build a signal fire and await rescue. While not the most elaborate of schemes, it sufficed to motivate me. Grabbing my walking stick, I slid down the embankment into the sandy wash to follow the river's edge. Here, out of biting distance from the crocodiles, I hoped to follow its meandering path to the road in relative safety. The river basin, generally between 75 and 100 feet wide, would afford me ample warning if any predators advanced. To expedite spotting the road, my plan was to hike five minutes, pop up to the top the embankment to scan for the track, and then return to the safety of the riverbed to continue on another five minutes.

The morning proved quite chilly when I started out, a mere fifty degrees Fahrenheit, but quickly warmed up as I lengthened my stride. Within minutes I observed a beautiful bird resembling America's bald eagle soaring sedately overhead, its white head tilted above dark wings as it scanned the river basin for prey. A scampering in the underbrush revealed a scrub hare with huge rounded ears that quickly, after catching one glimpse of me, dived back into the underbrush. Fifteen minutes later, a huge, slouching, dog-like creature materialized on the other side of the river. Joined by another, the pair turned curious heads toward me, studying me with small, round eyes.

The spotted hyenas, luckily for me, must have had a successful hunt the night before because they paid me little mind as they casually trotted up the sandy embankment into Mozambique. Thank God they were uninterested in me! It was amazing how I'd enjoyed the bountiful wildlife from inside the jeep much more than now. Almost immediately I spotted a beautiful gray and profusely hairy antelope with two oxpeckers clinging to his side. He drifted down to the water and daintily placed a slender black nose into the sluggish stream. Horns only slightly curved, his sturdy body was slashed with perpendicular white stripes, and he had a prominent white bar across his nose.

The bulky male nyala rested upon slender white legs and I recalled how the Australian tourists had mentioned how abundant the breed was in this area. How I longed for Peter's calm voice educating me about the nyala's habits, and tears rushed to my eyes again. If I could only touch him once again. I rested and watched the hairy buck for a long while until his timid mate joined him. Though plainer and lacking horns, she still proved exquisite. The male watched me intently as his mate tentatively stepped into the water to take a cool drink; he the ever-vigilant protector. Scanning the rocky debris lining the Limpopo River, I also decided it was time for a drink.

With the beautiful antelope standing guard for me, I knelt and partook of a long, refreshing drink before refilling my bottle. The hairy antelope drifted off with its mate in tow and once again I continued my quest for the road. A low, rumbling sound, similar to the kind a distant helicopter makes, intensified. Mystified, I at first clung to the vain hope that it might be a truck, until the sounds of stomping and snorting proved otherwise. Glancing about fearfully, with no idea from which direction the sound originated, I remained paralyzed. The dual embankments of the Limpopo River seemed to disguise the sound's direction as the rumble echoed across its wide corridor.

The ground began to shake beneath my sneakers. As its trembling increased, my survival instincts screamed for me to flee; but to where? Jutting from the nearest bank, a slight overhang of protruding brown rock beckoned. To its right a gentle slope eased down to the river, the grass beaten down to reveal a well-worn trail. Running to the rocky shelter I dove under the overhang to sit trembling as the earthquake-like rumbling increased. A horrible stench assailed my nostrils as the noise intensified to a roar.

A strong mixture of feces, flies, and animal mucus made me gag as the air turned rank. I dug trembling fingers into the crumbly soil as the first giant creature lumbered down into the wash just to the left of me. The massive male stopped and snorted, his curved horns shaped like some sort of monstrous headdress. Slimy mucus dripped from his nose and oxpeckers hopped impatiently upon his back. Weighing at least half a ton, he stood a good five feet high at the shoulder. His left ear hung ragged from previous violent encounters. The herd's forward scout remained completely rigid while slowly scanning the riverbank. I froze, scarcely able to breathe; terrified he would pick up my cowardly scent. I'd heard about the Cape buffalo's notoriously bad temper and prayed he couldn't spy me cowering inside my dusty hideaway.

I remembered Peter's tale of how Japanese tourists inside their car had been charged by a malevolent male who'd been guarding his offspring. He'd managed to gouge three good-sized holes into their passenger seat door, and they'd felt lucky to escape with only that minute damage. My throat convulsed as the dirty animal's massive shoulders gave a nasty twitch. He sniffed and searched the brush for several minutes before finally delivering a loud snort and lumbering on. Suddenly the rest of the herd followed, crashing down the embankment and slinging sand and gravel every which way as they plunged into the wash.

They converged upon the Limpopo River, so many pushing their way down the steep riverbank that the ensuing cloud of dust obscured them from sight. Every so often, as I held my sweatshirt over my mouth, the dust would clear just enough to reveal how the herd kept their young clustered tightly in the middle, with a larger male or female flanking them to keep the calves safe from predators. During this process, the shallow river water was churned into brown froth as swarming flies hovered above the advancing herd's mud-encrusted coats.

I've never seen a more awesome or frightening sight as those two hundred beasts crossing the Limpopo River. They progressed leisurely, only reluctantly surging up the other side of the embankment into Mozambique. The continuous noise deafened me, their attendant dust and flies appalling. The Cape buffaloes' rank smell easily penetrated the soft weave of my sweatshirt. I'd desired to view all the Big Five, and now had witnessed one of its most dangerous in fearsome mass. Finally, the last straggler scrambled up the sandy sides of the Limpopo River, leaving me huddled and choking in its retreat. Fresh piles of shiny black dung, similar to cow patties, dotted the river basin, over which hordes of flies already hovered.

The brown river water, now rendered unfit for drinking, had been churned to froth. As the dust cleared I saw a young crocodile, no longer than three feet in length, lying half on its back, one foot protruding above the foamy water. Bloody and trampled, a grotesque victim of the crushing hooves of the migratory animals, it now lay nauseatingly still in the muddy water. As I eased myself from the overhang, two crocodiles on outstretched reptilian legs slowly approached the corpse of the unfortunate youngster. I backed away and leaning upon my staff, watched them cannibalize their dead kin.

Crocodiles do not eat politely or daintily; they rip and shred their victim, tearing off huge pieces while violently shaking their scaly heads as they unsympathetically gulp down the whole bloody mess. The white expanse of their massive necks and throats convulsing and swallowing the meat of their comrade further convinced me of what I already knew; I had to avoid the river at all costs. Using the wide trail left by the Cape buffalo, I sidestepped several unsavory piles of black dung to scramble up the South African side of the river.

Distancing myself from the river by at least twenty feet, I struggled to remain parallel with the leisurely Limpopo. The sun finally offered some heat and I removed my sweatshirt, tying it around my waist. As the morning warmed I began to sweat, attracting annoying gnats that swarmed around my face. My insect repellant was still in my luggage at Shingwedzi camp. I remembered how Peter had suggested we take a night drive and mentioned we would only need the repellant then. That night drive was supposed to have been last night! I forced myself to continue moving, my progress miserable, as I batted futilely at the persistent pests.

I trudged on for what seemed hours before finally halting and sinking down upon a rotten log to watch two yellow-billed hornbills energetically hop from branch to branch in an umbrella thorn tree. I'd devoured my last energy bar, but still felt strangely light-headed. Overly sun-sensitive, I'd lost my sunglasses in the frenzy of my escape from the hijackers, and a throbbing headache now joined the fatigue. There was still no sign of the road and I had little clue as to where I was situated in regard to Crooks' Corner. The only certain thing was that the river remained to my right. Or did it? Damn my lack of directional sense! My scanty meal completed, I cautiously used the bushes before wearily continuing my laborious walk, concerned at the lessening pile of tissues remaining. I had to find civilization soon!

The next couple of hours were the stuff of nightmares. Hadn't I passed this same ragged thorn tree before? Wasn't that formation of rock almost identical to one I'd trudged by not ten minutes ago? A persistent pounding in my ears intensified with every step and every so often, an acrid scent assailed my nostrils. The sky had strangely darkened along with my mood and the bush seemed quieter, as if the creatures within held their breaths. The figs and acacias loomed particularly dense in this region and while lessening the midday heat, I fretted at my lack of vision.

I halted abruptly and sniffed. Could that be smoke I detected? My heart raced. It must be a campfire from a rest camp or picnic area nearby! I rushed through the brush, dazed and dizzy, but elated and hopeful. Just as suddenly as it had begun, the smoke brought to me by the benevolent wind ceased, the comforting smell no longer guiding my footsteps. The letdown was nearly as intense as the shock of being hijacked. The reality of being stranded in the bush took its toll and I again felt near weeping as my legs ached and my feet throbbed. In disgust, I stood cursing vehemently until the urge to cry vanished. I wouldn't allow myself to disintegrate into that trembling mass of dejected wimpy womanhood that modern Hollywood films and books portrayed. Mandy Phillips was stronger than that! Right now I might be hot and tired and slightly disoriented, but within a matter of minutes I'd find the road and soon after, be rescued and reunited with my Peter. I simply needed to sit down and catch my breath before continuing my sojourn.

Like all animals in distress, I sought shelter from the sun and found it under a rock overhang. Though small, not more than five feet wide, it proved adequate enough for me and cast a large band of shade. I scraped away the trash and pebbles and sank into the cool sand, pulling my legs up next to my chest in a defensive posture. Like a tortoise, I needed refuge and this hollow would suffice for the time being. The indentation was so small it wouldn't allow me to fully extend my legs, and I struggled to get comfortable. I hadn't meant to sleep, but after three big swallows of tepid water and the victorious consumption of two stray peanuts found at the bottom of my bag, I drifted away.

I couldn't know I slept for nearly three hours, unaware of encroaching danger. A harmless beige snake slithered near my nest, tongue flicking the air before retreating into the shadows. A brown and yellow ground squirrel, heartened by my lack of movement, dug frenziedly into the soil, its sole purpose survival. The midday sky glowed from a combination of sun and an advancing threat. The wind, suddenly shifting, drove licks of flame down the gentle slope, directly toward me.

Veldt fires are not remotely similar to the raging fires found in the Western United States. Here they are welcomed; their sluggish burning pace blackening the grass and replacing nutrients back into the soil to nurture the next generation. Controlled by fickle prevailing winds, they sometimes leave whole swatches of area untouched while completely scorching others. But I had no knowledge of these facts as I slumbered on, completely lost within the fatigue granted the weary and hopeless.

The ground squirrel's nostrils twitched and in a profound moment of awareness, she dove into her hole, safe inside the coolness of her newly-burrowed haven. I awoke abruptly, sinuses burning. Straightening, I clunked my head against the rocky overhang and let out a curse, my hand automatically rubbing the sore spot before halting in mid-air as realization dawned. The air glowed mustard brown as I fought to breathe. Bolting from my hole, I froze. The veldt was on fire! The flames licked steadily at the tall, dry grass which crackled noisily, warning the living to flee. A thorn tree to my left exploded; the ensuing smoke and sparks angrily reached for the sky. Behind me, more dry thorn and acacia trees waited patiently for destruction. The fire advanced, its flames in some places only a few inches high but in others, towering two to three feet. It howled and danced in victorious glee while rapidly consuming the tick-infested grass.

Where was I to go, what was I to do? Heart pounding, I pondered my feeble options. I could climb a tree, but after observing the nearby spiny trees being eaten by flames, I realized that option could likely turn into my funeral pyre. The second choice was to leap across the low wall of flame near my left, but the scorched earth would probably melt my Nikes. The blackened shrub, stretching as far as my eyes could see in the hazy air, still burned spottily in places. There was no telling where unburned ground existed and if I took off without rhyme or reason, I could become lost in the haze or succumb to the relentless, choking smoke. Just above the overhang, a small bush with milky pale leaves exploded, forcing me to duck for cover. Eyes stinging, I crouched like a trapped rat, seeking escape from the swirling smoke.

So this was how it was to end, then: Mandy Phillips consumed in a brush fire's relentless rage, her family, friends, and new lover forever pondering her fate. I brushed away a burning cinder and just by chance focused upon the recently-dug rodent hole. In a brainstorm I realized the tiny creature's survival instincts were my only option: I must burrow into the still-cool earth, squirreling myself away from the killer flames. My parents had owned a cocker spaniel that had died peacefully of old age at fourteen. Though spaniels are not known to be diggers, this black-and-white speckled canine had torn through every garden my mother had planted, her capable paws shooting the dirt behind her in a frenzied quest for bones. I dug like old Gurdie now.

My once carefully-manicured nails became the first victim of my relentless burrowing. A remembered piece of advice from a war movie—keep low and protect your back—propelled me. The heavy stone above would do just that. Soon I'd fashioned an eighteen-inch deep burrow and backed into it. Unzipping my canvas bag to use as a shield, I placed my sweatshirt over my face to cover my stinging eyes while setting my half-filled water bottle near me as a last stand against the approaching flames.

The air crackled, the flames occasionally roaring high in their superiority. The heat, intense beyond belief, caused my skin to redden and pucker like a Thanksgiving turkey. The hellish next ten minutes felt more like an hour. Another explosion from one of the trees above the overhang echoed, the reverberation from the heavy crash of one of its large branches causing sand to dislodge from the roots and shower down on my head. Ironically, throughout this entire Dante-like nightmare, I swear I heard the sweet trill of a distant bird. By the end of the firestorm I was coughing and grunting like a dying smoker, struggling to burrow even deeper into my hole, but never truly able to escape the black fumes. Finally the victorious smoke toppled me, my haggard body resting in a semi-stupor.

As suddenly as it had begun, the wind shifted and the flames died back on themselves. I roused gradually, still dazed and hesitant to leave the safe haven of my den. I waited a long time, the continuous crackle of trees burning in the distance reminding me of how fragile an escape I'd made. I emerged cautiously. The fire had claimed a strange t-shaped area. The swath to the left of my haven was untouched; the other completely scorched. Smoke swirled everywhere, but a quickening wind enabled me to breathe easily. An approaching sight forced me to quickly duck back inside my shelter. A solitary black-and-white spotted civet, sporting its distinctive black mask, leaped from one un-scorched spot to another, bounding more like a springbuck than the raccoon-like carnivore it was. This usually nocturnal creature had, like me, been awakened from its sleep to try and escape the fire. Once she missed her mark and howling, rapidly leaped again. A hundred feet below my haven, she finally struck cool dirt and loped off, her usually spotted fur smudged even darker from the soot. She never even noticed me and was, like myself, a survivor.

My neighborly ground squirrel poked its head from the hole fronting my burrow. I remained completely still and watched her sniff the air. Head cocked, the small mammal noted my presence and subsequently bolted straight back into her hole. I ignored the little creature's advice and emerged to observe the desolation around me. I could only imagine the sight I presented: jeans torn and stained, hands rubbed raw from digging, and my hair resembling the most despicable of witches. For some reason it all seemed quite funny and I broke into laugh. I laughed until I cried, and only stopped when my tears ran dry.

# Chapter 12

*I don't know exactly what forced me to start moving again.*
Maybe it was the severity of the scorched earth around me,
accompanied by my burning thirst that compelled me toward the
river. I'd drained my water bottle, but my throat still stung.
Before heading anywhere, I needed a refill. It took a good while
to escape the smoke and small areas of burning brush, and it was
only after twenty minutes that I encountered dry scrub again. The
faint gush of the Limpopo sounded in the distance and like a man
stranded in the desert, I forgot reason and sprinted for the river.
My staff held loosely in my hand, I plunged recklessly down the
embankment to finally kneel by the water and gulp wildly. When
sanity finally returned, I filled my bottle and rinsed my hands and
face. As I leaned over the water, my reflection revealed a
frightening, smoke-encrusted hag and I closed my eyes against
the sight of the bedraggled monster peering back at me.

It was with renewed determination that I returned to my old
plan of following the river in hopes of eventually running into
Crooks' Corner. Nothing seemed as straightforward as before. I
felt weak and nauseous—possibly from the effects of

contaminated water—and my feet dragged. Another irritant set in as hunger gnawed at me, and I felt strangely achy and dizzy. To keep myself going I made up another of my stupid, mindless tunes. *Find the road and it'll take you home, find the road and it'll take you home.* The chant seemed to work as I staggered up the bank to follow the gentle bend of the river.

I would have been surprised to learn that I actually sang the words and perhaps it was that inane song that kept the predators and snakes away. Or maybe, far wiser than I, all sane creatures had vacated the area because of the fire. I tried alternating walking fifteen minutes and resting five. All the peanuts, biltong, and energy bars were soon gone and my stomach echoed like a hollow drum. A headache brought on by hunger coupled with the persistent glare of the sun nagged at me, and I found I needed rest stops more frequently.

I didn't run into much wildlife. A petite yellow mongoose scampered across my trail, and gigantic black ants scrambled over a boulder. A group of five or six buzzards soared dizzily overhead and I heard a strange clacking sound in the distance, but other than that it seemed like I traipsed alone in the bush. Mentally I kept making calculations. Certainly I must come upon the road sometime soon, since it ran parallel to the river. But where was it? I teetered and stumbled more and more as the minutes stretched into hours. Gradually panic set in. I knew I'd been disoriented by the fire and the snake, but I couldn't have totally lost track of my whereabouts, could I? Could I?

Damn my miserable sense of direction, anyhow! If I'd half the sense God gave a toddler, I'd have relocated the road by now and reunited with Peter, relating to him wildly embellished details regarding my torturous night in the bush. But no, here I trudged, perspiring, hopeless, and light-headed, alongside a riverbank from hell. Almost done in, my head jerked upward toward the faint roar of an engine. It took me less than two seconds to determine it was a helicopter. Exhilaration followed the thought that Peter was likely spearheading the search for me!

Ascertaining it would be difficult for rescuers to catch sight of me in the underbrush entangling the riverbank, I plunged down the sandy cliffs into the relative openness of the river. The chopper's engine churned, violently shaking the tops of the trees. From where I stood shouting, I could barely make out that it was a military helicopter. What resembled a camouflaged leg dangled out the door and I glimpsed the barrel of a rifle held in ebony hands. They appeared to be on the hunt of something, and I sincerely hoped it was me. I waved and hollered, but the helicopter didn't approach any closer.

Yanking the sweatshirt from my waist, I flapped the gray jersey in the air, hoping to flag them down. Suddenly the helicopter swerved, zooming back to the South African side. A burst of gunfire filled the air, followed by the high-pitched shriek of an animal or human. Fool that I was, I bolted toward the direction of the gunfire, still convinced that those in the helicopter would save me. I jumped over half-buried logs, swerved past thorn trees with inch-long spikes, and startled a few speckled ground birds resembling fat quail as I pursued the diminishing hum of the helicopter.

So reckless was I that a thorny branch smacked me in the face, tearing the corner of my mouth as I hurtled through the bush. They were getting away! The chopper, now only a dime-sized speck in the sky, could scarcely be heard above the hum of the river. I abruptly pulled up, my staff no defense against the revolting sight greeting me. I'd seen photos of such inhumanity before, but had never witnessed such a thing first hand.

The rhino lay deathly still, its feet tucked awkwardly under its slack torso. The heavy, still body lay half-tilted toward the sun, already bloated and grotesque, flies swarming about the bloody hide. The poachers had cut off its horn; the matted, crimson stump was already turning black as the blood dried. Their victim had been shot twice point blank in the head and my heart ached to see such an awesome animal brought so low. Not far from the corpse, deep tire tracks, probably from the poacher's truck, had scored the earth as the murderers sought to escape. Just beyond the clearing a half-dozen or so vultures hopped about, impatiently waiting for me to back off. The smaller, white-backed ones squabbled amongst themselves while two others, much larger and dirty-brown colored, eyed me. They were prepared, I guess, to fight for the carcass. The poachers had most likely been spotted by the helicopter as they performed their greedy surgery and fled, the military pursuing them through the concealing brush.

In despair I realized the helicopter hadn't been searching for me at all but had been hunting the scourge of the game parks: the poacher. I wilted there in the hot, bright sun and sobbed. I cried not only because I was hungry, hot, lost and alone, separated from Peter, but also because of the gruesome horror inflicted upon such a beautiful animal for the supposed medicinal power hidden inside its horn. I sank down upon my knees and wept like there was no tomorrow.

I didn't notice the shadow falling across my anguished form.

"Mandy?" grunted a raspy, familiar voice.

My head jerked up and there he stood, carrying a thick, hand-crafted spear instead of a rifle.

Peter lunged for me and I wept in earnest, my arms tightening in a choke hold around his neck.

"Peter! Peter, I was afraid you were dead!"

"But of course not, my dearest."

"You found me, you found me!"

"Actually, only by the purest luck. I've been searching for you ever since those bastards abducted you." He glanced about nervously. "Did you see them?" he asked, stroking my dirty hair. "Are they close by?"

I peered past where he stood in a blurry effort to identify those others he referred to.

"Who?" I asked dumbly.

A peculiar expression crossed his face. "The poachers. The army helicopter was chasing them."

That minor fact just wasn't that important. "You're alive. I was afraid…"

"I know, I know my darling. But we can't talk now. We need to get away from here."

"But the helicopter… we've got to wait so it can rescue us!"

"No, Mandy. They'll think we're poachers and shoot us. We've got to move away from here and quickly. They will shoot first and ask questions later. Trust me. We've got to get out of Mozambique and back to South Africa."

"We're not on the South African side? We're not close to Crooks' Corner?"

Peter pulled at my arm and I allowed him to lead me away from the desecrated rhino. "Crooks' Corner is completely in the opposite direction from here."

I gazed at him blankly. "No, it isn't. It's just up there to the north a ways. I figured if I kept following the river, I'd hit it or the road in a few minutes."

"I'm sorry to disagree, Mandy, but Crooks' Corner is to the *southwest*. You're in Mozambique and that helicopter was full of

South African soldiers tracking down poachers. Mozambique turns a blind eye to the SA army crossing their borders for a little 'man-hunting.'"

How could I have gotten so turned around? What Peter said was inconceivable. "But I was following the river," I repeated obstinately.

"The river meanders like one huge snake. It took a sharp turn about two kilometers back and we, and the river, are now inside Mozambique."

Peter paused to scrutinize me and I glimpsed the sparkle of humor in his dark eyes.

I could only imagine that unsavory vision with my hair falling out of its ponytail, clothes filthy and torn, and my anxiety barely held in check. I grasped my walking stick, color burning my face. Luckily the soot from the fire, mixed with blood from my torn cheek and mouth, disguised my blush. I must have resembled something a mangy alley cat might drag home.

Peter pulled off his safari hat and placed it upon my head to ward off the burning sun. He gently pulled at my arm again. "You tell me your tale later, but now we've got to keep going." It was only then that I noticed he limped painfully and the fingers on his right hand were blistered.

"You're hurt," I managed.

"It's nothing. I got burned when I climbed a tree to avoid the fire. I can't believe you're safe." His voice broke a bit as he picked up the pace, his limp more noticeable. We trudged, silent for nearly fifteen minutes before Peter hesitated at a large outcropping of rock. He gingerly sank down in the sand, taking me with him.

I couldn't stop the floodgate of tears and Peter, wise in most things, let me weep, cradling me in his arms. Nearly ten minutes later, I hiccupped and wiped my face with my sooty hand. He smiled crookedly and suddenly I felt reassured. A huge, dark millipede crawled near his boot and I jerked.

"Don't fear the *shongalolo*," Peter said. "It is perfectly harmless. "Now tell me everything that happened."

I kept it as brief as possible. "This African man approached and mentioned he'd seen fresh lion tracks nearby. He grabbed me and pulled me from the jeep and started waving a gun. The hijacker commandeered the 4 x 4, and another white van followed us as they drove down a road parallel to the river. I knew they were going to kill or rape me, so at the first opportunity I managed to escape. I spent the night alone in the bush. You'd laugh, but I did manage to make a fire. This morning I encountered a herd of Cape buffalo crossing the river and afterwards was so tired that I fell asleep and a fire crept up on me. And then the rhino." I paused, searching for words sufficient enough to describe my awful experience. "That's all."

My statement seemed so inadequate for all I'd been through that I was certain Peter would ask for more details, but my brief recital satisfied him. He was smart enough to visualize the rest. "How wondrously brave you were," he finally said, pride brightening his dirty face.

My breath caught. Me brave? I managed, "And you, I swore I caught a glimpse of you running parallel to the river right after I was hijacked."

"You did."

"Tell me," I urged.

A frown settled upon his haggard face as he draped his arm across my shoulder.

"One would think I was a rank amateur to the bush, Mandy. My first mistake was leaving the rifle in the jeep. No one in their right mind goes into the African bush without a firearm. And then…" His pause was poignant. "And then I spied a river monitor. They're awesome creatures and I couldn't resist heading down to the river to catch a closer peek. That noble gentleman was nearly a meter long from his tail to his nose and I watched him a good five minutes before Mr. Monitor hissed at me in indignation and sauntered away. I'd just started up the embankment when I heard voices and realized I was too far away to thwart your hijacking."

"They would have killed you."

"It's highly likely," he said wryly. "When they tore out, I started running. My reasonable, guide self ordered me to remain at Crooks' Corner where I could flag down another vehicle and notify the authorities. But the other, more emotional part of me propelled my legs to follow you come hell or high water. If I lost track of you, I felt, no one would ever find you."

"They meant to rape and kill me," I confirmed shakily.

"For sure. I figured if they stayed to the dirt road, I'd have a fighting chance, but when they struck out into the deep bush there was no question about pursuing you."

"I knew you would do all in your power to find me."

"Luckily, the terrain was rough and their vehicles couldn't proceed very quickly. It's a miracle I didn't run into any big game—I only startled a bushbuck in my mad dash. I tried to take a shortcut at a small rise and spied the two vehicles just below me. And then you did the craziest, bravest thing I've ever seen. You jumped from the jeep. I would have yelled bravo if I hadn't spotted a pair of hijackers lighting out after you, guns blazing. I skirted them and was, at one point, within 100 meters of thug number one when he winged his own comrade. I crouched behind some shrubs and by that time, you'd crossed the river. You didn't even notice the crocs and hippos." He laughed mirthlessly. "My daring lady just ran for her life."

"They seemed much friendlier to me at the time. And then what happened?" I urged.

"I skirted the hijackers and scrambled down the embankment to the river, right into a small bramble of acacia bushes. A thorn penetrated my boot and even though it was bloody agony, I continued. I crossed the river downstream from you. I was so certain I'd happen upon you, but after a few minutes it became evident that if I didn't stop and remove the thorn I'd be in serious medical trouble. It was a nasty one."

"So that's why you're limping." I stated.

"I've washed it out a few times and can only hope it isn't infected. By the time I was able to move on, I couldn't find you. It seemed like you'd disappeared off the face of the planet."

"I hid in a tree."

He laughed. "Go figure. I should have realized you'd do just that, since you harbored such a fascination with 'leopard' trees."

"And, I made a fire."

He stared at me in admiration. "You did? That's wonderful."

"It was not my best 'Girl Scout' moment. It took five tries. I thought... I hoped... maybe someone would glimpse it."

He knew what I meant. "I didn't. When darkness fell I had to find some shelter. I dug myself into an overhang similar to this and waited out the night."

"No fire?"

"Ach, shame... no matches." He flashed a dirty lop-sided grin. "I did have a meal, though." Peter touched the hunter's knife he always wore on his belt. "The aqama was mighty tasty, even if I did eat it raw." At my horrified expression he added,

"Builds character, eating it uncooked. I swore I heard you early the next morning."

I shook my head. "Perhaps...?"

"I'm positive I caught a glimpse of your pullover near the road. I heard a crashing through the bush and I headed in the direction of the sound. Something charged through the bush and left the road. I was certain you'd stick to the road."

The memory of that morning flooded back. "The snake," I gasped.

"Snake?" Peter's face turned serious.

"There was this huge snake with a black mouth that looked like it had a smile on its face... and... and it chased me for ages."

His brow furrowed. "A snake that smiled? Interior of mouth black?"

I nodded. "Yes, it was this enormous gray serpent that reared up in the road. It must have been twice the length of me, and I swear it pursued me."

Peter said wryly. "It appears you encountered Mama Mamba."

"Mama Mamba?"

"The black mamba. The children at grade school called her Mama Mamba. Her mouth perpetually fixed in a smile, she's one of the deadliest snakes in Africa. No wonder you fled. She chases her victims and one drop of her neurotoxic venom can kill a grown man in less than sixty minutes. It shuts down the muscles, including the lungs, causing one to suffocate. You were fortunate indeed."

I gulped painfully. If I'd known how dangerous the snake really was at the time, it probably would have been a heart attack, not the serpent that killed me.

"We were so close!" I moaned. "Then what happened?"

"I kept marching on, my foot killing me. I doubled back to the dirt track, hoping that by a miracle you'd stumble upon it again. I didn't like the fact we were in Mozambique."

"Why?"

"I know it doesn't seem like it, but the infrastructure in Kruger is far superior to Mozambique. Finding assistance is easier on the South African side of the river. Also, well—people from Mozambique are not fond of white Zimbabweans. Even if they realized I wasn't a poacher, they might just kill me on principle, since many sympathize with Mugabe."

"Why?" I asked, confused.

"Zimbabwe used to be called Rhodesia, and both it and Mozambique were formally ruled by the minority whites. Mugabe used the fact that most whites oppressed the native Shona in Zimbabwe as an excuse to seize power. The farms were grabbed and many died, including my uncle who was shot on his plot. The irony is that Mugabe hurt the Shona more than the whites. Lots of black Zimbabweans cross Kruger into South Africa in hopes of finding work. Their economy has failed under Mugabe. He should have followed the model of South Africa, where the races worked together for a common good."

"Because of Mandela?"

"Yes, Madiba. The grand unifier. He's the reason I came to South Africa in the first place. Both Botswana and South Africa succeeded at putting aside their ethnic hate. So, I chose South Africa to live. Anyway, just as I became positive I'd located your trail, the fire erupted."

I remembered the horror of the licking flames and my desperate burrowing into the sand like a frantic squirrel. "Your hand. That's when you hurt your hand."

"The wind-driven flames cornered me, so I climbed a tree that had already burned at the base. I grabbed a still-smoldering branch and this was the result."

I gingerly took his damaged right hand; the palm torn and blackened with second- and third-degree burns. "I wish I had some aloe to smooth on this. So how *did* you finally locate me?"

"The 'copters. I was so chuffed, as I believed they were searching for us. I only recognized it held South African troops on poacher patrol a bit belatedly. Hearing gunfire, I dove for the bushes and prayed you'd hear the helicopter's motor as well. I reckon the third time's the charm, because here you are."

"And here *you* are." I lowered his sandy head and kissed his lips tenderly. "So now what?"

"We must cross the river and return to South Africa. Once we find a road, we should locate help." He smiled. "I must say I'm partial to your stick."

I shook it a little. "It's my defense against hungry varmints."

He smiled ruefully. "Well, between your staff and my spear and knife, I reckon we're quite safe."

His playful words cheered me. "You're my good luck charm, Peter," I stated bravely, rising.

I brushed off the clinging sand, adjusted Peter's hat over my tangled hair and gripping my staff, followed him to South Africa.

I had escaped death three times with the herd of Cape buffalo, the smiling snake, and the raging fire. Though too incompetent, too out of control, and too uneducated in the ways of the bush to survive, I'd somehow lasted the night and the better part of a day. Now, I felt totally optimistic. Peter appeared to as well, though he limped badly and I sensed his hand pained him.

A bird with a long, slightly-curved bill, its erect crest dabbed in black, alighted on the ground near us as we headed for the river. It possessed a body colored an enchanting cinnamon, and its striped black-and-white wings made the small bird unforgettable. It poked at the sandy soil only a few feet from us. At our disturbing approach, the brightly-colored bird hopped in alarm and cried *hoop, hoop, hoop,* before jumping crazily into a nearby thorn tree.

"Did you see that beautiful bird?"

"I did." For some strange reason, Peter laughed heartily.

"It's the *pupupu* or common hoopoe, lass. It's found everywhere, whether town or bush. Many believe it brings good luck and dreams, with positive omens of the future. You brought that bird with you, didn't you, Mandy Phillips?"

I smiled. "Of course I did, Mr. Leigh."

He halted abruptly and grabbed me roughly by the arm. "Now, you listen carefully, lass, and promise me you'll do exactly as I ask."

"Anything," I said.

"Walk directly behind me and only step where I step. If I order you to freeze, you freeze. If I command you to run, you run. You don't wait for me or argue with me. Do you understand?"

"I promise."

"That's my brave girl. Let's hope the luck of your hoopoe continues on our trek."

# Chapter 13

*I thought Peter would take a direct path to the road, but* instead he meandered through the bush, keeping his eyes peeled and remaining cautious on his path. I remembered my own earlier haphazard flight through the bush and observed his progress closely.

He paused after a few minutes and gestured to a heavily-leafed tree. "Do you recognize this tree, my lady?"

"I really don't have a clue. I'm not very good with plants." Peter pointed his makeshift spear at the grayish-brown bark.

"This is called the common hook thorn, and it's the most populous tree in the area."

I moved forward to examine its twisting trunk. At least eight meters high, it provided lush shade. Interspersed among its drooping foliage, ample thorns in lethal pairs warned browsers to beware. I reached a hand up, glad to pause under its blessed shade.

"Careful," warned Peter. "You must look before you reach. Within the tree's branches might be anything from a serpent to a leopard. Some trees even have blistering agents. It's better to be cautious."

Peter then touched a small tree whose healthy leaves were shiny and thin with hair-like tips. They drooped slightly upon a long stalk.

"This is a bead bean tree. The pods are eaten by many animals, but unfortunately taste nasty to humans. I don't know about you lass, but I'm famished. We've got to find something to eat."

It wasn't more than thirty minutes before I began to flag, my energy nearly spent. My stomach refused to stop growling, unfed after my mid-morning splurge on peanuts and the remaining energy bar.

A large, spreading shrub we passed held countless long flowers resembling faded yellow trumpets and though I wished to inquire about the pale blooms, Peter seemed preoccupied, his eyes continually searching the rough terrain. He paused, his head cocked at an angle, before nodding to himself.

"How are you holding up, milady?"

"Okay," I said bravely.

"That's the spirit."

I trudged in silence after him, trying to take note of my surroundings. Peter halted abruptly and I nearly ran into him.

"There." He pointed and amazingly, the wide Limpopo River stretched before me.

"It can't be," I protested. "The river was directly behind me. I swear it was behind me!"

Peter shrugged his broad shoulders. "Many say the Limpopo is deceitful like a snake, twisting this way and that. And, like the serpent, it will lure you to its treacherous shores. We have to be cautious now; there are crocodiles everywhere."

I followed Peter down the sandy bank and gingerly stepped over some tortured logs, thrashed about by the unforgiving summer storms.

"Check out that fellow," he said, pointing to a yellow-tailed crocodile that lay sunning himself. "This one is lazy and no threat, for he's eaten not long ago and just wants to bask in the sun. Better, though, to give him a wide berth. Come this way, lass; crocs can move more quickly than you can imagine."

Here the river trickled slowly, so low it lapped below my knees. The coolness felt wonderful after our hurried pace, and I stooped to quickly fill my two-liter bottle after splashing some water upon my hot face and neck. After climbing some bright boulders, we stood upon the other side of the river.

"Welcome back to South Africa," Peter said.

I'd never felt happier in my life. "I don't see any crocodiles about. Why don't you remove your boot and let me take a peek at your foot."

Peter hesitated and I thought he was going to refuse. He finally nodded and sank down upon a log near the lapping water. Gingerly, he removed first his bloody sock, then shoe. I knelt before him and examined his foot. Black blood had congealed over the wound and the edges appeared raw and red.

"I think it could do with a washing."

"Righto," agreed Peter and placing a hand upon my shoulder, limped to the water. He rinsed it as thoroughly as he could in the murky water and then hopped back to the log. I pulled off the sweatshirt tied about my waist and dried his foot.

"I wish I had something to bind it with."

"Does it appear infected?"

"I don't think so," I said truthfully. "But walking on it can't be beneficial to the healing process."

"Well, since I don't have much of a choice, let's get this show back on the road. Um, perhaps you'll want to wash your face, Mandy."

His wry smile took me by surprise.

"Is it that bad?"

"Looks somewhat like military camouflage," he said lightly as I bent and splashed water on my face.

"Much better," he declared, and within a couple minutes was back in the lead, reshod and, to my mind, limping less.

"Do you have an idea where the road lies?" I asked.

"It's to our left, only a couple of kilometers away. We must hurry to reach it before dark."

It was rough going, but I made sure I never once complained. Peter set a good pace, and I didn't want to let him down.

Breathless and annoyed by the countless bugs swarming around my face, I didn't see the road until were finally upon it. The dirt track lay dry and dusty. Not ten feet from where we stood, a huge pile of dung lay gently smoking in the sun. A red-billed hornbill poked around the dung, searching for insects.

"I know this slip road," Peter said quietly. "It's closed to tourists, but if we continue up it a couple of kilometers, we should run into the junction that leads to Crooks' Corner. Once there, we simply turn left and head toward Pafuri. Left would be best because so many cars come that way."

I grinned happily as we set off briskly, giving the huge pile of fresh dung a wide berth. My heart soared. I could almost see my camp and feel the softness of our bed. But first, first, I would give the park rangers the license plate number I'd scribbled down. It wouldn't be long now!

The service road curved slightly to the left and we strode quickly, already feeling the coolness signaling that evening was set to arrive. As we rounded the corner I stopped short in terror, stunned by the sight of the huge bull elephant directly in our path.

"Damn," hissed Peter under his breath and raised his arm, warning me to stand completely still. The pachyderm took an excited step back and raised his trunk, letting out a tremendous trumpet. His huge ears flapped and he elevated his right foot, just like a Spanish bull does before preparing to charge. I stood paralyzed, my heart chugging like a freight train. The elephant trumpeted again and took a heavy step forward.

Peter whispered. "Move back very slowly, Mandy."

The gigantic herbivore lifted his trunk and smelled the breeze, his ears flapping wildly. Taking one tentative step backward, then another, we slowly distanced ourselves from the irate male. Just when I believed we were safe and had nearly reached the curve of the road, the bull let out a gusty roar and charged down the dusty track.

We turned tail and ran for our lives, plowing through the heavy underbrush, me screaming at the top of my lungs. The elephant crashed after us, bellowing and snorting. I ran faster than I'd ever run before, but the elephant still gained on me. Peter, even with his damaged foot, sprinted a meter ahead. The snort of the elephant's heavy breath sounded behind me and I realized it would only be a matter of seconds before he'd trample me to death. In desperation, I veered sharply right. Suddenly I was jerked off my feet and thrown to the ground. A ringing noise and choking dust made it hard to focus or hear, but the sensation of being rolled across the brush and shoved inside the roots of a dead tree made some sort of jumbled sense.

A hand covered my mouth and Peter hissed the word "quiet" in my ear.

Our refuge was a termite hill built around the roots of a huge, dying tree that had been kicked in and abandoned at some earlier date. Peter's heart pounded next to my back and I didn't need his urging to remain completely still. The elephant snorted roughly and sucking sand into his trunk, propelled it like shotgun pellets into the air. Jumbo then turned his rage upon a nearby thorn tree, using his versatile trunk to grab a branch and rip it off. The selfsame tree then received countless tusk thrusts as the pachyderm vented his spleen on the now shredded and uprooted tree.

I have no clue as to why the bull elephant never located us. I just remember watching in petrified fascination as he scouted the area searching for us, using his trunk like a bat to swipe at the underbrush. The heavy pads of his broad feet sent little puffs of dust into the air and occasionally, he bellowed his ire. After a long while, the rogue male finally moved away. A lifetime later, Peter whispered into my ear.

"It's lucky Master Elephant has such poor eyesight or he would have discovered us for sure."

We stayed that way, tightly crouched inside the enveloping roots and red soil of the mound, until the late afternoon again became filled with bird and insect noise. Peter gave me a quick hug before urging me out of our sanctuary. Filthy with dirt and twigs embedded in my hair, I swayed in front of the copper-colored termite hill and tried vainly to remove the sticks and leaves. Peter shook his head grimly. My staff had fallen to the ground near the mound, and his crude spear rocked in the slight breeze where it had been thrown into the root mound of an acacia tree. He spoke quietly and contritely.

"It's my fault, Mandy. I knew the elephant dung to be fresh, but headed in that direction anyway. I'd hoped vainly he'd already moved off the road, but I should have known better. Only two weeks ago, a man crossing from Mozambique was trampled to death when he got in the middle of a herd near the river. Elephants are dangerous and unpredictable; you never know what they're going to do. Our friend here was an old rogue male nearing sixty years of age."

I gulped and gazed at my hands. They were shaking. "I thought elephants travel in herds?"

"Usually they do, but often the old rogues are forced out because of their belligerent behavior. He's likely on his last set of teeth and doesn't have much time remaining. Not being able to chew and digest the foliage he needs, *Kambaku* is hungry and irritable."

"His last set of teeth?" I stammered. I suddenly envisioned the elephant having serrated rows of teeth like a great white shark I'd seen on the *National Geographic* channel.

"Yes. Remember at the elephant museum in Letaba when I mentioned how the elephant has only six rows of teeth in his lifetime? He lives to about sixty and dies after his last set wear out. Basically, he starves to death. It's nature's way of culling the herd. Can make an old chap like that highly irritable."

Peter took my hands and gently rubbed my palms with his thumbs. "We're going to be okay, Mandy. Someday, this will be quite an adventure to tell our grandchildren."

I couldn't disguise the joy in my eyes. The laugh lines around his mouth twitched as he wrenched his spear out of the dirt.

"We must hurry just now if we stand any chance of getting to Crooks' Corner before sunset."

# Chapter 14

*The elephant had unnerved me more than I cared to admit,* so Peter switched to the role of game guide as we walked, in order to distract me. When a high-pitched *kee-kee* sounded above me, Peter gestured toward a small eagle circling silently. A light tan color with a shadowed head and dark wings underneath, the raptor released a high-pitched cry.

"That's a booted eagle, very common and found everywhere. Loves to eat rodents. Ah, hear him now; he's screeching *peee-peee-peee* because he's on the trail of something. The mongoose better beware."

Peter motioned toward a huge, barrel-shaped tree with strong, entangled roots. "That is one of the most common trees in Kruger: the wild fig. It casts deep shade in the summer. And that tall one there… that's a shepherd tree and has wide velvety leaves. And there's another common hook thorn like I pointed out earlier."

I'd made acquaintance with several of these trees before, but hadn't known their names. "Why do so many trees have thorns?" I asked, pointing at the sharp pairs of dangerous barbs.

"It's a tough life," he shrugged. "Everything wants to eat something else. The grazers and browsers want to consume the trees and the shrubs and unless the vegetation finds a way to keep the majority of the predators away, they perish. So trees like this form thorns. However, the giraffe and selected others can still pluck the leaves daintily from between the barbs. That's why most trees use tannins as their best defense to keep from being browsed too much."

"Tannins? I've heard of that somewhere. Doesn't it have something to do with tanning hides?"

Peter whirled, his teeth bright in his dirty face and very clearly pleased. "That's right. Early settlers and tribesmen learned to remove tannins from these trees to cure their hides. I'm surprised that you know that, my lady."

"I think I saw it on a nature show once," I stated sheepishly. "But you were explaining about the tannins."

"Yes, well these trees have tannins inside their stems, bark, and leaves. When a tree has been grazed too much, the tannin level rises, causing the browsers to dislike the foul taste and move away. It's one method the trees use to save themselves. It's crucial that they flower and create berries and seeds.

It was almost as if trees could think. I tucked this amazing fact away in my brain. I stepped gingerly over a fallen log and then started. A mass of large brown bugs similar to ants scurried over the rotting surface.

"What are they?" I asked Peter.

He moved closer. "Just termites. They made that convenient mound we hid in while the elephant rampaged. Termites exist everywhere in the park. As you can see, this tree has been disturbed recently, which provoked the termites. They dislike light. In fact …" His eyes narrowed. "I want you to remain here for a moment, Mandy. I need to check something."

Holding a tanned hand up to shade his eyes, Peter quickly scanned the dense woodland.

"Aha," Peter said. He pointed solemnly to the ground and I saw large heaps of finely formed black dung, clods the size of a fist. It was scattered everywhere, and I noted that the surrounding vegetation had been trampled down.

Peter glanced at me and shook his head. "This is not good."

The shiny dung seemed familiar. "What is it?" I asked, crossing my arms protectively across my breast, my suspicions raised.

"The Cape buffalo. They've passed here not more than an hour ago. Their dung is just now being infested by beetle and fly."

"Can we go around?"

"Perhaps. I need to determine what direction they're heading. Hopefully, they're not making for the river."

"That must be the herd I noticed crossing the Limpopo earlier."

"Then you understand the danger." He gazed at me keenly. "You know they're one of the Big Five, so named because they're one of the most dangerous animals to hunt. Any self-respecting trophy hunter must bag a Cape buffalo from Africa. They generally occur in large herds, often spreading out over a couple of kilometers as they migrate. It's too easy to run into a solitary male or bachelor herd and then big trouble follows. Once, while driving a pair of German tourists, an angry buffalo chased after my jeep for over three kilometers. The Germans believed it great fun, never recognizing the danger. Cape buffalos are very irritable creatures."

"Just like that rogue elephant?"

"Yes, but he had an excuse. He has a toothache. Cape buffalos are mean for meanness' sake."

I sank down upon a log, but not without first examining it. "So, what do we do now?"

Peter wavered before sighing. "Wait here, lass. I need to scout around. It wouldn't be wise to be caught in between parts of the herd."

Peter searched the bushes and laid my large stick next to my feet. "I'll keep the spear if that's okay with you?" he asked politely.

I nodded, understanding.

"I'll be back just now," he stated before disappearing into the bush. When the minutes ticked ominously to twenty-five, I started to panic. Certain I needed to defend myself, I picked up my staff and rested it across my knees, my fidgeting churning up the dirt between my feet.

I observed many birds and creatures while I rested there in the partial shade of the thorn tree. One black-headed, long-tailed little creature hopped up not three feet from me, giving a long, trilling *trrrrrr* noise similar to an alarm clock. It had an orange face and shaggy crest, and I wished Peter was there to identify the noisy rodent.

Later, a couple of yellow-billed hornbills came and picked at the dung, dispersing several beetles as they searched for edible bits. A chestnut bird that reminded me of a finch hopped from branch to branch, and a few rusty-breasted birds I felt certain were swallows darted between the trees. For a moment, a wave of homesickness swept over me as I remembered the swallows that gathered mud to make their circular homes under the eaves of my so-distant condominium. It was chilly here in the partial shade and I missed the warm sun of Florida, with its broad, expansive beaches. But what I missed most that vanquished sense of security. I was no longer firmly in control of my life.

A long millipede passed less than six inches from the toe of my trainers and disappeared behind my resting knapsack, but I decided that if I didn't bother it, it wouldn't bother me. What had Peter called it—a *shongololo*? A couple of times I heard a crackle in the bush and sat very still, hoping it wasn't a hungry predator. Where on earth was Peter? I glanced at my wristwatch. It had been thirty minutes!

Peter finally appeared, acting like he'd been gone no more than five minutes.

"I was starting to get worried." I complained like a nagging wife. "You said you'd be right back."

"Did I? There's a very large herd of Cape buffalo spread out over a couple kilometers and moving away from us. It's very likely part of the herd you encountered earlier. They're heading for the water, but unfortunately doing so at a very slow pace. We need to switch direction and skirt the back of the herd. I don't wish to run into any of the impatient young males who've formed bachelor groups at the rear. They're frisky and unpredictable."

I remembered their frenzied plunge into the water as their thrashing hooves churned up crocs and mud. There was no way I wished to face any of them on foot. Rising, I nodded and shouldered my backpack.

"You're hungry," he acknowledged, the pinched look on my pale face making it a fact. I nodded solemnly.

"I have just the thing for two hungry wanderers. Think you could make a fire again?"

I smiled. "I still have some matches."

"I'll gather some wood."

The nearly smokeless fire sent up an almost invisible wisp of vapor into the trees. By the time it had risen above the fig and thorn trees, it was rendered indiscernible to the human eye. My stomach rumbled noisily as I watched in fascination as Peter removed his hunter's knife and started working on the two huge yam-like roots he'd dug up. He trimmed off the sweet potatoes' skins competently before slicing the root into flat hamburger-sized patties and folding them inside large leaves. He shoved the yams under the flames. Immediately, they began hissing.

Peter had speared a small muskrat, which he skinned efficiently before suspending the small carcass over the fire, turning it every so often. A wonderful odor soon filled the air. Now, I've never been very fond of sweet potatoes, always passing up that particular proffered dish at Thanksgiving and Christmas, since I avoid carbs at all costs. But as Peter cut the muskrat's flesh sparingly into small bite-size pieces spread over the now-smoking slices of yam, I had to admit I'd never smelled anything more appetizing in my entire life. Our plates consisted of two large flat leaves from a branch of a small bush.

Peter dusted them off on his pants and held one out to me with a flourish.

"Your plate, ma'am." He stabbed a sweet potato and lifted it onto my leaf, proceeding to stack three additional steaming slices, one atop the other.

"They will be very hot," he warned before sitting down in the dirt to eat, breaking off pieces of his own yam with his fingers. It was the most delicious thing I'd ever tasted. The yam, cooked through and filled with rich flavor, perfectly complimented the muskrat, which added protein. I passed Peter my water bottle, the water tasting much fresher and cleaner than before. Whether it was my acute appetite, or Peter's comforting presence, I felt great.

"Do you notice the spoor of the buffalo in the dry mud?"

I leaned toward where he pointed. Indeed, several clear imprints existed, a good two to three inches long and pressed deeply into the soil to reveal the creature's massive weight. Two blunt horn impressions facing each other resembled a domestic cow's hoof print.

"Only one?" I asked nervously.

"As far as I can tell, a big one. Perhaps eight hundred kilograms or more."

Eight hundred kilograms. I did a swift calculation. If there are 2.2 pounds to a kilo, then... I whistled. The Cape buffalo weighed in at a hefty 1,700 pounds. I gulped. At 120 pounds, I was no match for Mr. Irritability.

"So," Peter said, wiping his greasy hands upon his khaki trousers. "We must travel a bit more before making camp."

"Camp! Camp? But I hoped we were going to reach the road." I tried to keep my voice even, but failed.

He pointed to the sky, whose light had suddenly faded. "Within less than an hour it will be dark. We'll walk to where there is water and set up. We don't have much choice, Mandy. We can't get around the buffalo in time to reach the road and flag someone down. It's nearly sunset."

My face must have shown my anguish. "But I want to get back now! I can't spend another night in the bush!"

Peter's warm eyes found mine as he reached for my hand and gave it a squeeze. "We're going to make it, lass," he promised quietly before adding lightly. "You know, people pay me damn good money for walking safaris like this."

"I know," I said shakily. "And you're worth every dime." We gazed a long while at one another before he leaned forward and lingeringly kissed my chapped lips.

He reluctantly pulled away and added mischievously, "I suspect it *is* probably best we know one another a sight longer before I meet your mother."

Blood suffused my face, before I managed a grin. The thought of Peter sparring with my mother lifted my mood considerably.

"I need to go over *there* for a second." I groped around in my backpack for the last remaining Kleenexes and leaned my walking stick against a crumbling gray log.

"Beware, sweet lady. There are red ants whose life's pleasure is to wait for squatting women so they can sting their bottoms."

I giggled and stalked off. Peter called after me. "When you are finished, wait by the acacia tree. I'll scout out the area, which will give you an illusion of privacy."

I moved away as far as I felt was safe and squatted over a small indentation in the sand. This time it was easy to go. It's amazing how twenty-four hours in the bush takes away your modesty.

I waited impatiently by the acacia tree, noting the air had turned chilly. While Peter was correct about not traveling so close to dusk, I'd so much have preferred a hot bath and warm, shared bed. Lost in that pleasant fantasy, I started when the late afternoon suddenly burst open in a frenzy of movement.

"*Shumba!*" Peter cried.

He hurdled over a downed tree, a lioness not a hundred yards behind him. Peter sprinted full speed, Olympic quality, his knees tucked high like the best hurdler. I watched, powerless to alter the massive feline's burst of energy. Peter cast a frenzied glance over his shoulder and I recognized the cat was gaining. I had a choice. I could either stand by like all those helpless women in fairy tales and male-dominated movies I'd despised forever, or I could do something.

My staff rested near my backpack, out of reach. I searched the brush and grabbed a thick, dirt-encrusted stick. It was covered in thorns, but I scarcely registered the stabbing pricks as I raised it above my shoulders. A member of the softball team in high school, I still played with the local women's league whenever I found time. Bat held ready, I lunged forward to where the lion advanced at breakneck speed. It was now or never. The beast was so intent on her prey, she must not have seen me. I swung, putting every ounce of effort into the blow, and managed to strike the huge feline directly across the muzzle. The satisfying crunch of her nose crumbling under the force of the blow filled the late afternoon air.

The lion flipped before jumping backwards as agilely as a house cat, roaring hoarsely as her paws sought wildly to remove the thorns now embedded in her broken nose. She whirled and fought the stickers, half-blinded in the process as she frantically battled the unseen force that had nearly knocked her senseless. The cat staggered before running off in the opposite direction, crashing wildly through the deep bush, her yowls and intermittent roars expressing her acute agony.

Amazed, I watched the tawny feline disappear into the underbrush. The end of my makeshift weapon had splintered with the force and now tumbled from my numb fingers. I scurried over to the log to scoop up my walking stick just in case she returned. Peter had completely disappeared and I searched frantically for him. Two hundred meters away, perched in what he later informed me was a false thorn tree, he watched my approach. He had bounded into a tree, as agile as the cat that chased him. Peter rested upon his haunches, his mouth forming a perfect O. While the blood trickled from my punctured hands, his words reverberated through the trees.

"You crazy American! You could have been killed. Why didn't you run to safety?"

"Didn't feel like it," I stated, staring defiantly at him in a mixture of anger and love.

Peter stiffly jumped down and slowly dusted his hands on his filthy trousers before lifting his eyes to mine. "That was the craziest, most spontaneous act of courage I have ever witnessed in my life and I will never, ever forget it."

He moved forward to lift my bleeding hands to his lips. "What a pair we make," he murmured, and for the longest while, neither of us spoke.

Later, as I thoughtfully followed Peter, placing my feet methodically inside his every footprint, I realized that no matter what happened, I would never be the same. That wimpy, trembling Mandy no longer existed, and a real man—warm, capable, and intelligent—respected and cared for me. It was an epiphany.

Cautiously, Peter pointed out the numerous round piles of Cape buffalo dung littering the area. It took us the better part of an hour to finally skirt the main herd. Once, I heard a couple of males snorting in the dense thicket not far from us, and Peter froze before forcing us to back up. He finally paused at some bushes covered in dense, hair-like strands of spider web. I was as breathless as if I'd run a race, my jeans streaked with blood from the countless times I'd tried to wipe my oozing hands clean.

"Unfortunately, we are now very far from the road. It will be dark soon and we must locate a safe place away from the lions and the Cape buffalo, but still close to water."

I trusted him implicitly and this time did not whine about another night in the bush. "What do you suggest?"

"If my memory serves me correctly, there's a water pump not that far from here that was built to generate water for the wildlife in the dry season. We'll be lucky if we make it by dark. I'm concerned, however, that dangerous creatures use the water generated by the pump." He glanced up at me. "Are you strong enough to hike three more kilometers?"

"I'm not tired," I lied.

Peter stared up at me for a long moment. "You broke that lioness's nose," he stated quietly. "I suspect you could trudge all night if needed."

"I could at that."

"Then let's move; we have little time."

# Chapter 15

*As we tromped through the brush, occasional thorns* dragging at my jean-clad legs, I noted the clear air turning rapidly colder. I paused long enough to pull on my sweatshirt, though Peter never seemed to tire or grow cold. The khaki legs of his dirty trousers moved rapidly and methodically in front of me. Within ten minutes or so, we managed to merge with an animal trail and stuck to it, even though Peter mentioned it could be more dangerous. Strewn along the trail, small piles of nut-sized pellets littered the narrow path.

He smiled. "*Mhara* or impala walked this way."

Twice we stopped abruptly. Once a huge male waterbuck, the bull's-eye on his hairy rear providing a moving target, bounded skittishly away at our approach, its straight, grooved horns so sharp they were often lethal to a lion. Another time, Peter halted and grabbed my arm, clearly excited.

"Look," he directed, "near the termite mound. There's a sight you'll rarely see."

It was nearly dusk and I hesitated to stop, knowing how vulnerable we were on this heavily-traveled trail. At first I could discern nothing except for a flock of dark birds pecking at the mound. Before long, however, I distinguished a nearly hairless, humped figure with a short tail crouched in the short brown grass. It dug rapidly at the termite hill. The creature lifted its head, its dark eyes seemingly not noticing us. Possessing long, jack-rabbit ears and sharp claws, I was at a loss to identify it.

Peter leaned forward and whispered in my ear, "You are fortunate indeed, lass. That is an aardvark. He's nocturnal, few ever notice him, though other animals like the hyena, porcupine, and jackal love to take ownership of his abandoned shelters. He is a famous digger. His presence warns us the sun is nearly set."

"Shouldn't we be there by now?" I suggested hopefully.

"Soon," he reassured. "We must find enough wood to light a fire. The night animals are beginning to stir."

"Isn't the leopard a night animal?" I asked nervously.

"The best and the most beautiful. But he prefers riverine valleys. Quick, lass."

We left the shy aardvark and continued upon the animal trail until, less than five minutes later, he pointed at something that made my heart leap. A windmill turned slowly in the faint breeze, pumping water to fill a two-meter long trough. The flat, dry area around the waterhole appeared vacant except for a small flock of guinea fowl, whose blue heads flashed and ducked as they hunted for insects in the short grass.

"Now that we made it, I'm not sure I'm partial to this place," said Peter after a while.

"Why not?" I asked, quite relieved to see the manmade pump.

"It's too open and unsheltered. It makes us vulnerable. Keep a sharp lookout and stay by the trees over there. I'll fetch some fresh water and search for dry wood."

He moved briskly, grabbing my water bottle before hurrying to the trough. Bending, Peter rapidly filled it, his head jerking nervously to each side. I started. Not far to the right of him, a large pile of bones stank in the sun. A partial ribcage, skinny leg bone, and hairy skull were all that remained of some unfortunate antelope. From where I stood, I noticed small pieces of dried skin clinging to the joints, though the rest of the carcass was picked amazingly clean.

Peter hurried back. "There's been a lion kill here, not more than twenty-four hours ago." He pointed to the skeleton I'd noted. Twenty-four hours! That was all it had taken to reduce a living creature to that?

"Because we're inland and away from the Limpopo, this waterhole is used by many animals in the evening hours during the dry season. It's best we find shelter and make a fire where we can watch the waterhole from a distance."

"Is there a road close by?" I asked.

He shook his head. "Not now. Many of these tracks have been abandoned as Kruger Park officials seek more and more to not damage the environment. Pity."

We spent the better part of a quarter-hour searching for a sheltered place until Peter finally found a spot that satisfied him. A rock outcropping with the roots of a dead old tree hanging overhead extended eerily toward us. Using his spear-stick, Peter poked into the soft soil beneath to reveal an old burrow. He sniffed and prodded the opening before giving it his seal of approval.

"Whatever lived here before is long gone. We should be safe. If we build a fire, our backs will be protected."

The dusk rapidly approached and I shivered. Without being told, I quickly gathered small sticks and kindling and then handed Peter my matches. There were only twelve left. I could only hope he was better at starting a fire than I. His tinder caught alight with the first match and I heaved a huge sigh of relief before cautiously gathering up some dry grass to soften our bed.

"You always do that," said Peter, leaning upon his spear to watch me work. "You make sure the bed is cozy for us. I like that."

"And I like your fire."

The fire soon blazed and I settled down upon a log Peter had dragged over, stretching my chilled fingers toward the blaze. Already the temperature had dropped by at least five degrees Celsius since he'd filled my water bottle.

"My fire smoked and one log reeked," I said.

"You probably found some stinkwood. It is most foul when burned. Mandy, after I leave, if you hear anything, stand up and do your best to make yourself appear big, swinging the stick. I'll be back soon."

"Where are you going?" I said, the idea of him straying more than twenty feet away suddenly terrifying.

"I figured my lady might be hungry."

I nodded guiltily. It had been a long time since the wonderful lunch of yams and muskrat. Peter swooped up his spear and bent over me, giving me a husbandly peck on the cheek, as if he were only just running to the local grocery store, before disappearing into the trees. I knew better than to beg him to stay. My new Mandy was not clingy or demanding.

I sat by the fire for over an hour. The sun abruptly vanished and the night dropped like a curtain. Suddenly every shadow, every rustle in the bush seemed a threat. Where could he be? What was taking him so long? My gnawing hunger soon transformed into blatant concern. What if something had happened to him? What if he'd been attacked by a lion or bitten by a snake or fallen down and broke his leg? Where would *I* be without Peter?

Little more than an hour after he'd disappeared into the scrub, a monstrous shadow loomed from behind the fire. I shrieked and leaped up, my stick held ready.

"That's my girl! Always on guard!" Peter laughed. "I've brought us back some supper; a little suni."

The small antelope's neck tilted at an odd angle. The beautiful little buck possessed miniature horns and couldn't have weighed more than ten pounds. My stomach churned in revulsion or, more likely, sympathy as Peter dropped the tiny, beige creature upon the ground.

"Mandy, why don't you rustle me up some sharp, dry sticks so we can roast the meat?" He said quietly, eyeing my stricken face.

I lingered on the edges of the campsite for nearly ten minutes before returning. Thankfully, Peter had made short work of cutting the carcass into three sections. He reached for the long, sharp stick I handed him and thrust three big pieces of meat upon it.

"Lean it at an angle over the fire to start roasting the meat. I must dispose of the rest of the carcass."

"But won't we need some… some of the rest for breakfast?"

Peter shook his head slightly and once again I realized my idiocy.

"If we leave the carcass here," he explained, "the hyena, jackal, or even lion might haunt the fringes of our fire, hoping to scavenge some meat. I must remove the remains to a distant area and let the scavengers have their dessert."

He was gone in an instant, lugging the suni's remains inside the poor beast's skin while I pretended not to look. I made a show of planting the stick with our dinner at an angle, in an effort to prop it up securely. Within a matter of minutes the heavy chunks started to roast, dripping fat onto the hot fire which spat viciously at me, forcing me to dodge. Peter returned in a matter of minutes, his hands and face wet.

"There were no animals at the waterhole, so I washed myself in hopes of removing the smell of dead flesh." His eyes crinkled as he critically observed my efforts.

"If we leave the meat so low over the flames, it will probably scorch. If we could somehow move it higher. Let's see . . ."

Peter loped into the bush and returned with two stout V-shaped sticks. He propped the heavy skewer, laden with the meat, atop the Vs to make a spit. The cut-up carcass now hissed a good foot above the flames.

"Just keep turning the stick slowly and soon we'll have roast suni."

It was a Spartan meal that night, consisting only of the half-cooked flesh of the tiny deer, followed by tepid water. It was, however, enough to remove the dreadful ache in my innards.

"You're tired, my lady," Peter said gently as I leaned back against the rock, my stomach now full.

"Very," I admitted. I pointed to the stars. "Those make a lovely ceiling."

He glanced upward. "Indeed they do. No stars like this where you live?"

"Sometimes. But I live inside the city limits and its lights dim the brilliance of the stars. Here, there is nothing to interfere with their beauty."

I searched for the big dipper before it occurred to me that it might only be discernable from the Northern Hemisphere.

Nevertheless, the stars warmed me. I felt so much more comfortable this night than the previous.

"Come here," urged Peter and I moved closer to him so he could once again drape his warm, comforting arm around my shoulders. I leaned my head into his shoulder and felt almost content. Suddenly I stiffened. From not far off came the deep, low roar of the lion, followed by an answering call. My fingers drifted to my walking staff where it leaned against our log.

"Will the lion find us here?"

"I buried the suni's entrails far enough away from the watering hole that scavengers should leave us alone. If we keep the fire burning high, we should be fine. It's crucial we sleep between the rock and the fire so no animal can approach us without first braving the flames. Are you frightened, my lady?"

"Yes," I admitted honestly. "But more relaxed this night than last. When I was a child, my grandfather and I would lie out and gaze at the stars. I've never seen quite so many before." A mosquito buzzed near my ear and I swatted at it, laughing. "It's hard to believe that there are still mosquitoes this time of the year, when it's so chilly at night."

Peter smiled and poked at the dancing fire. "They are generally gone, so luckily for us, the scourge of malaria has died out by winter."

I shivered and hugged my arms to my chest, staring moodily into the fire. The mosquito remained persistent and I slapped fruitlessly at him between my hands. The nimble insect took warning and instead buzzed around Peter's head. A wave of depression settled over me.

Peter must have noted my mood, for he said lightly. "My father was a great storyteller. I remember one tale in particular regarding this whining mosquito. Would you like to hear it?"

"Alright." It was better than brooding about what dangers the night concealed. Once again, the lion bellowed her low, searching roar and I shivered instinctively.

Peter didn't begin until he'd given the fire another vigorous poke. "In the old days there were no electric fences to keep the lion away, and the people shivered at night just like you do. We told stories in the dancing flames to keep those things we didn't understand or that frightened us at bay. Take that mosquito who buzzes in your ear. He has always been very annoying—since the beginning of time—and do you want to know why?"

I nodded like a rapt child.

"Mosquito whines in your ear, even in the winter when he should have been frozen and dead, because he is trying to make you understand his side of the story."

I laughed. "He has a story to tell, then?"

"But of course. All creatures do. We just don't want to listen."

I smiled as Peter launched into his campfire tale.

"Long ago, the mosquito was whining and buzzing as usual. This time he picked upon the poor iguana. Iguana was busy changing colors, you see, and became annoyed at the mosquito's constant buzzing. Finally, fed up, he put sticks in his ears so he'd not have to hear the mosquito's constant whining. Iguana shuffled away, thankful that he could not hear mosquito anymore."

Peter peeled some bark off a dry stick and tossed the pieces into the fire, taking his own sweet time to relay the story.

"Unfortunately, however, the iguana didn't realize he couldn't hear anything. Now, the python who rules the ground said 'Good morning' to his friend the iguana. He had always admired the lizard for his brilliant colors. But because of the sticks in his ears, Iguana could not hear the python and walked right on, mumbling to himself. The python was upset at being ignored, so he angrily slithered into the ground.

"The burrow he entered was a rabbit's hole. The rabbit knew that whenever a snake entered its burrow, death soon followed, so the rabbit quickly bounded out of the other exit, frightened and shaking. He ran through the reeds, scared out of his wits. A shiny black crow witnessed the rabbit running and was certain something horrible chased the hare. He squawked out a loud *caw-caw-caw* that echoed through the jungle. Vervet Monkey sat in the trees, grooming himself. At the frightful cawing of the crow, he scrambled up the old thorn tree and jumped onto a thin branch. Sadly the branch broke, knocking into an owl's nest where a baby owlet slept, killing her instantly. Mama Owl became so sad, it was dreadful. It's a dangerous thing to make an owl sad, you see, because she has the most important responsibility of all the animals. Do you know what that is?"

"What?" I whispered, fascinated by the simple tale.

"It's the owl's job to wake the sun. The owl is a night creature with huge eyes, but as her eyes grow sleepy, she hoots and makes the sun rise. But this night, since Owl's eyes were filled with tears, she did not hoot. Darkness reigned over the land for several days and the sun never rose. Soon, King Lion, who struts majestically across the veldt, became very angry.

"'Where is the sun?' he said. 'I wish to lie under it and raise my paws toward its welcoming rays. But alas, there has been no sun for three days.'

"So he demanded a grand council and all the animals assembled, except, of course, for Owl. Upon hearing the tale of Mama Owl's woe, Lion sent Leopard to fetch Owl from her hole in the spiny thorn tree. When she arrived, her big eyes were round and wet.

"'Why did you not waken the sun?' demanded the king angrily.

"'I shall never waken the sun again, for you see, the monkey climbed on a branch and a dead limb fell down and crushed my baby. Now that she is dead, I no longer wish to see the day.'

"'*Rrooaaar*,' let out the lion, who had a mighty temper. 'Therefore it must be the monkey's fault.' But the vervet monkey jumped up and down, his gray fur trembling in fright at the huge lion's roar.

"'It was not me! It was not me! I only bounded up the tree because the crow gave alarm. It's his job to warn us of danger!'

"Crow spread his wings, his large black beak pointing into the air indignantly. 'It was not I,' he cawed. 'I only gave the alarm because the rabbit was running through the bush. Something frightful was chasing it.'

"The poor scrub hare shook in fear as the lion's yellow gaze turned upon it. 'It wasn't me,' it squeaked. 'You see, the big rock python slithered into my burrow and I had to run for my life.'

"The lion turned to the huge, reticulated python. 'And you? Why did you slither into the rabbit's burrow? It is clear you caused all this mess!'

"'Not I,' hissed the rock python indignantly. 'It's all because of the iguana. I said good morning to him—he's my best friend you know—and... and he *ignored* me.'

"'Go get iguana,' roared the lion. The warthogs rushed off and rounded up the poor lizard. When he appeared in front of the king of the beasts, all the other animals began to laugh because, you see, sticks still protruded from his ears.

"'What are those for?' the lion asked, but Iguana, of course, couldn't hear him. Finally, the vervet monkey hopped over and shaking the iguana, plucked one of the sticks out of his ear.

· "'So you're the one who caused the owl to forget to hoot for the sunrise,' accused the lion.

"The iguana appeared startled and then changed color, so deep was his shame. He miraculously turned from green to yellow and then pink. 'It wasn't me,' he stammered. 'It was that mosquito. He was whining and whining and buzzing in my ears and finally, to shut off his annoying hum, I put sticks in my ears so I wouldn't have to listen to him anymore.'

"The lion could not help but roar with laughter. 'Bring forth the mosquito!'

"But the mosquito, who often lurks unseen, had heard all and quickly hid among the reeds in the marsh.

"'Oh dear,' whined the little mosquito. 'I'm in big trouble now!' So great was his fear that he only came out at dusk and the early morning, so no one could see him.

"'I am very sorry about your owlet,' said the lion to Owl, once the mosquito's story had been told. 'Please, promise me you will hoot for the day to break. Hopefully, by doing your duty, you will be granted another owlet to help dry your tears.'

"Owl obeyed her king and when she hooted, the bright sun came out, filling the world with warmth. But it is quite true that to this day the mosquito still feels he has been wronged and whines in your ear every morning and evening to tell his side of the story."

# Chapter 16

*I clapped my hands in delight. "That's a wonderful story,* Peter!"

"I have heard it told many ways. The Shona often sing it in repetition, but I thought you would prefer if I didn't turn your ears into stone with my horrible voice."

I laughed and gave him a sweet kiss before thrusting my hands closer to the fire. "We used to sing songs and tell stories around the campfire at Girl Scout camp," I said huskily, longing for the security of those carefree days.

"I was speculating," suggested Peter wisely as I scratched viciously at his mosquito bite, "that your fiancé resembled a mosquito in many ways, sucking you dry before throwing you away for fresher blood. Some men are like that."

"My mother didn't see it that way. She thought I should have stayed in Florida and joined a dating service."

"And instead you embarked upon that honeymoon on your own, met me, and were hijacked. My sister believes everything happens for a reason," said Peter. "Thus, it was your fate to come here. Each person has a destiny and you were meant to travel to Africa."

"Perhaps."

"Mandy…I knew the first time I saw you at The Vineyard that you'd change my life for the better. I *believe* in fate."

I peered up into the glorious heavens as an unseen night bird tittered in the bush only meters away. As the brave fire flickered, I took his hand and lifted it to my lips.

"I believe in you Peter."

We sat for a long, contented while before Peter threw his prodding stick into the fire and using my bag as a pillow, indicated the place in the grass-lined sand for me to lie.

"Will you join me?" I asked hopefully, only desiring to once again hold his lean body close to mine and make love to him.

"I'm afraid I must keep watch for a while and plan our route for tomorrow."

Disappointed, I lay with my back to the fire and wished its warmth was Peter before drifting away as the sounds of the night bird and crackling fire merged into nothingness.


I awakened to discover Peter adding wood to the fire. My glowing watch revealed it was not even five. I itched all over and, dreadfully uncomfortable and thoroughly chilled, stumbled to the rough log by the fire.

"You get some rest?"

"Some, though I'm incredibly sore. You sleep?"

"A bit," he responded, returning my hug. "We're in trouble, Mandy. We've got to find a road and fast. Luck has been our best friend, but it's bound to run out soon. It's a miracle I found you, and a bigger one that you survived all you've been through. Just think about our luck with the lioness. Generally she would have hunted with a pride, but most likely, this time she hunted alone for her cubs. You saved me, Mandy, but the question is: can I save you?"

I hadn't ever imagined Peter would falter.

"We've come so far," I declared. "We'll reach the road and find assistance. I can feel it." I reached for his hand but hesitated when I noticed that his burns, while less inflamed, still oozed from several of the popped second-degree blisters. He followed my eyes.

"We're pretty beaten up, eh lass? To complicate issues, the lions have been active tonight and a hyena was pacing outside our campsite, just in the shadows. The grim reality is I don't have a rifle, we've no additional food, and poachers lurk in the vicinity. We've *got* to obtain help and fast."

I had sensed it all along, but since reuniting with Peter I'd always believed we were close to rescue.

"You rest, Peter, and when the sun rises, we'll set out and find that road. We're weary and overwrought, but think about what we've overcome—poachers, snakes, lions, Cape buffalo. I'm not going to give up on you or us, ever. Get some sleep and when it's light we'll begin our last leg of this grand adventure.

Peter stared at me for a long while before depositing a light kiss upon my cheek and warmly hugging my stiff shoulders. He reoccupied the indentation in the sand I'd vacated as I added more wood to the fire. An owl hooted in the distance and a strange, high-pitched cackle cracked the air. I flinched and pulled my staff nearer. Peter did not rouse. Determined, I kept watch over my newfound love and freedom.

# *Chapter 17*

---

*Dawn had barely spread her orange glow across the sky* when Peter stirred, stretched, and scratched his bristled chin before smiling at me.

"Howzit?" he asked sleepily.

"Fine. I, um, really have to go to the bathroom, but unfortunately, all my tissue's used up."

Peter chuckled, rose and strutted to the edge of the fire's glow, pulling at some tree before returning.

"Here, your Majesty."

"What is it?"

"It's called the weeping wattle. It has soft leaves and stems. Many Africans use it as paper for their toilet."

I reluctantly took the soft wad of leaves and hurrying around a dark shadow of bush, did my business. I could hear Peter foraging about at the edges of our camp as I returned to the fire and placed another graying log upon its low flames.

"Bingo!" he chortled and soon presented, just like a grand chef before his best client, a handful of pale-tan eggs nearly the size of chicken eggs. I watched as he quickly set a flat rock near the fire and cracked four of the eggs upon its gray surface.

"How did you find them?" I asked as I gathered my battered backpack that had served as our pillow and retrieved my Swiss army knife with its small, retractable fork. My stomach rumbled in anticipation.

"Several fat guinea fowl were scratching in the clearing, so I poked around the outskirts to discover their clutch and raided the nest. They're almost ready. We must move soon, before the animals gather for their morning drink."

Peter used his knife expertly as a spatula and dished all four upon a wide leaf.

"What about you?" I asked as used my little fork to jab one of the cooked eggs into my mouth. Its searing heat forced me to gasp and suck cool air.

Peter laughed. "My four next. And here's something *really* special." He shoved a dirty, blue sports bottle towards me. "It was half-buried in the sand. I'll scrub it out at the watering hole and we'll have another drinking container!"

His mood had perked up considerably. Chewing another egg cautiously, Peter cracked the final four upon the scraped rock and leaned back upon his heels. A small black and yellow bee buzzed near his head as the egg yolks slowly hardened.

"Thank you," I said quietly as he scooped one of the cooked eggs into his mouth.

He seemed perplexed. "For the water bottle or the eggs?"

"For those, of course. But... but for caring enough to continue searching for me even when it seemed hopeless. To brave the bush with only... only your sharpened stick and a knife. For... "

"Hush, lass," Peter ordered, instantly at my side, both arms about my now-shaking frame. "You would have done the same for me."

"Yes," I agreed. "But no one has ever cared about me enough to risk anything... ever." I stared down at my filthy backpack, heart pounding.

"It's all because of Disneyland, you know," said Peter thoughtfully after a time. I gazed at him, bewildered. "I only chased after you because I was certain you could secure me some free tickets to Orlando."

"Oh, really?" I said shakily. "And it's Disneyworld in Florida, not *Disneyland.* That theme park is located in Southern California."

"That's what I meant. And of course, there are the Everglades. You'll be my guide in the Everglades, hey? I hear fearsome creatures inhabit the swamps, like alligators, invasive pythons, and venomous water snakes."

I laughed. "I'm afraid the most fearsome creature residing in Florida is my mother."

"Precisely. Then this jaunt will make good training for whenever I meet her. One cannot be too prepared."

I took his burned hand in my own. Amazingly, it seemed much better; its puffiness had diminished significantly over the past twelve hours. I cleared my throat awkwardly.

"Then I'd better get hold of those tickets, hadn't I?"

"Lekker! Up and at 'em then. Let's go find that road and hope the buffalo have dispersed."

# Chapter 18

*The buffalo herd had not completely moved on; a few males* still lingered and foraged. For thirty minutes we delayed, swatting persistent flies and gnats while waiting for them to disperse, their ample dung an irresistible draw for the pesky bugs. I sank onto an uncomfortable rock to wait the stray bulls out. Finally, the herd's grunts and groans lessened. When I tried to say something, Peter lifted a finger to his mouth to effectively silence me. My heart began its runaway freight train routine. A lion or a leopard or, in the back of mind, a stray ornery Cape buffalo must be near! He moved a cautious finger as I slowly turned my head.

Two small, alert creatures sniffed the air. The closest lifted its mustard-colored head and waved it from side to side, analyzing me as a possible predator. A short, deep-throated warning growl caused the second to cock its head as well, waving it up and down in a rhythmic dance-like movement. I remained stock-still, no longer afraid, but fascinated by the slender mammals.

Deciding we weren't a threat, the sun-basking weasel-like creatures began hitting their slender hands against branches to dislodge seeds before picking them up gently to chew upon. Every so often, their dexterous fingers grabbed a small branch again and battered it against the ground, the seeds zinging into the air as they dislodged. In a flash, the wily pair popped the kernels into their mouths. Holding their white-tipped tails upright, they alternated between crouching and standing erect like humans. Finally satisfied the small shrubs could offer them no more succulent seeds, they bounded off, disappearing under an umbrella of overhanging leaves.

"What were those?" I asked, dusting off my hopelessly soiled jeans.

"The yellow mongoose. Do you know that it rarely drinks, gaining most of its moisture from the dew on plants, the blood of insects, or the natural fluids from seeds and such? Once I witnessed a group of mongoose attack a cobra. The snake reared, but the mongooses lunged and snapped at the snake, distracting it. So many were they that finally the smallest one managed to grasp the snake's hood without being bitten. The mongoose bit straight through the cobra's head, and the pack later dined on his body. Quite amazing creatures, are they not, my lady?"

His calm tones and the way he was so clearly charmed by the little yellow mongooses served to deepen my love for him. I admitted it to myself now. I'd fallen hopelessly in love with Peter Leigh. His fascination with the rhythms of nature and everyday life endeared him to me. Even though we were lost in the bush, he still revered all our surroundings revealed to him. Whether it was the merciless lion or the energetic mongoose, Peter remained in balance with nature.

"I can barely hear the buffalo now," he said. "It should be safe to move in five minutes." He sucked on his new bottle before mentioning nonchalantly, "There was a pride of lions at the waterhole last night."

I clutched my staff, my hands trembling. "Th…there was?"

"Yes, but they had caught a young wildebeest far away from the fire and weren't interested in us. I didn't tell you since you would fret. I think, however, that we need to be very cautious since more lions than your poor old Broken Nose wander about."

As we set off again, I sidestepped massive deposits of buffalo droppings and noted a few huge, dry, deteriorating piles of elephant dung nearby. It had been several days since elephant had passed this way. Strange how, after only a couple of days in the bush, I was becoming attuned to its ways. The reassuring presence of Peter, armed with his hand-crafted spear, enabled me, as I traipsed directly behind him, to focus on the beautiful day around me. Only a chilly twelve degrees Celsius, the warmth of my pullover felt marvelous. The sky gleamed azure blue, cloudless and breathless, not a whisper of wind pulling at the dry branches of the shrub mopane. Small brown birds flitted here and there, making high trilling sounds as I followed the crunch of Peters's boots. At his query, I lengthened my stride to catch up with him.

"Did you know," he asked as I caught up, "that not far from where you were hijacked there is a SAPS post?"

"What is that?" I said, not certain to what this particular South African acronym referred.

"A South African Police post, not ten kilometers from Crooks' Corner."

I halted abruptly. "The police were that close?" I sputtered.

"Of course." Peter halted and eyed me, his dark orbs amused. "What better location than at the border near Crooks' Corner?"

His laughter cracked the morning and sent a pair of gray and pink doves diving for cover.

"Because they never got rid of all the crooks?" My smile was grim.

"Yes, as you unfortunately discovered. A notorious ring of hijackers operates out of Maputo, with ties to the north. I must say you were lucky to get away with your life. Very lucky."

"Why don't we head back toward the post?"

Peter paused a second too long. "Too much danger of being glimpsed by your very kidnappers. And the police are constantly roving the bush searching for poachers and those who cross illegally. Besides, they're an unruly bunch."

I thought his terminology strange. "What do you mean, they're an unruly bunch? This is the South African police. They're here to protect us."

Peter gave a descriptive shrug as somewhere to our left a black-and-white bird warbled merrily.

"They are not here to *help* us, Mandy. They're here on poacher patrol. After the opening of the tri-park borders, many refugees and poachers have tried to cross into Kruger. Both the soldiers and police shoot first and ask questions later. While I'm certain that they would not harm you, they'd have very little sympathy for me."

"I don't understand," I said. Peter was a ranger and guide. What was the problem?

He fidgeted and picked at a short shrub, breaking off a dead twig and commencing to chew on it. "I didn't wish to tell you this last night, but there is a rogue white poacher named Ian Voorhurst who leads a particularly nasty poaching ring. His nickname is 'Little Mouse,' since he's quite the wily one. Voorhurst is about my age, coloring, and build. " He paused significantly.

What he inferred took a while to sink in. I protested. "But you're well-known in the park!"

"To many of the guides perhaps, but only a couple in the SAPS would recognize me. Normally I'd be armed with my jeep, identification, and rifle. The anti-poaching squad is large and they wouldn't know me. There's a real chance they'd mistake me for Voorhurst, shoot first and ask questions later. We need to be very cautious of *any* armed group."

"Certainly *someone* must know you're missing?" It was almost a plea.

"My sister Elizabeth is aware that I'm on a job in Kruger. I generally don't stay in contact with her much while inside the park. Your travel agency knows where I am, and I registered in Letaba that I was guiding. No one would know you and I are missing, though. So we can only hope that when our room was not reoccupied, some of Shingwedzi's camp staff would notice and send out an alert."

I swallowed, trying to appear brave. "So what's the plan?" I whispered.

"We continue on our way and hope to run upon the road. But Mandy... "

"Yes?"

"If something *precarious* does happen, promise me you will look after yourself—don't worry about me. It's crucial we get you back to civilization and in the hands of the proper authorities."

Peter's intense brown eyes scrutinized me and I felt certain there was something more he wished to state. Silence loomed between us until I nodded reluctantly. Satisfied, he turned and began picking his way through the brush.

A rustle sounded to the left of me. It might simply be a small sand lizard burrowing into the deep band of shade, or it could be something else, like the Mama Mamba I'd encountered on my first day. Defenseless against my fears, I trailed behind Peter zombielike, scarcely noticing the startled leopard tortoise, who stuck his head protectively inside his shell, or the bemused vervet monkey who scratched his belly as I scurried through the bush, a rain cloud dampening my previous elation at discovering that I loved him.

# *Chapter 19*

*The monotonous trudge seemed to go on and on.* I ached, I itched, and I fretted. Peter seemed impervious to any of my anxious thoughts, setting a brisk pace that soon had the sweat trickling down my back and between my breasts, soaking my dirty top. I wrapped my sweatshirt around my waist, tying it in a tight knot below my belly button. Occasionally it caught upon a low thorn bush and dragged at me.

After a particularly vicious struggle, I removed the only protection I had between the chill of the evening and me and stuffed it into my knapsack. By this time Peter had surged way ahead of me, only the muted green of his cotton shirt flashing between the thick shrubberies. Having to trot to catch up, I hopped over tricky roots, carefully watching my step in fear I would land flat on my face.

So intent was I that I nearly ran into him. Peter had halted, watching the bush intently, his frozen body and still manner indicating some sort of creature lurked directly in front of us. It was then that I spotted the giraffe. An adult male, dark in color, it towered at least four meters tall. I'd never before considered giraffes dangerous and whispered, "Should we take cover?"

Peter shook his head. "Watch, Mandy," was all he said.

The dark reticulated giraffe backed himself up against a tall tree with grayish-white bark, whose leaves still remained faintly green during this dry season. The giraffe leaned heavily against the rough bark and, moving up and down, scratched himself violently against the rough bark of the tree. A few moments later he repositioned himself, this time running his long neck up against the tree trunk. I could hear the scraping sound from where I stood.

"Why is he doing that?" I murmured.

"Likely ticks or other parasites. Giraffes usually carry oxpeckers on their body. The birds remove ticks, but for some reason this old fellow doesn't have any attendant birds. He's horribly itchy, you see, and must scrape desperately against the bushwillow for some relief."

I could commiserate with the poor beast; my legs were driving me crazy.

"Do you notice how black his patches are?"

Indeed, I had never observed a giraffe as dark as this one. "Why is that?" I panted, still out of breath.

"He's very, very old. And look there," he pointed. "Something has taken a bite out of his left leg."

My eyes traveled down the giraffe's elongated body to where a huge scar and indentation distorted his sleek lines.

"We will leave this fellow to his back-scratching," Peter stated. "But be on the lookout. Giraffes usually travel in herds and while not considered dangerous, if they have young they can be quite protective. I heard a tale once of a giraffe kicking a man to death who had stupidly approached a nursing mother and its baby."

We gave the angular animal a wide berth and even though I kept my eyes peeled, I saw no further evidence of more giraffe.

"Beware of that plant, Mandy, it is the buffalo bean. Do not touch, please."

"Why?" The climber in question had long, velvety pods.

"The hairs on the pods are extremely irritating. If you brush them you will regret it for many hours, since the golden hairs are almost impossible to remove. I once made the mistake of picking some for my mother because I thought they were food. My hands were inflamed for days." Peter's commentary concluded, he once again strode ahead.

I dutifully followed, beginning to feel downright miserable. My parched throat made it difficult to talk and I noted Peter's soaked shirt, indicating he was probably extremely thirsty as well. To worsen matters, tiny gnats swarmed around my sweaty face. I swatted at the persistent pests, who were obviously attracted to my perspiration. Suddenly the iron bar of Peter's arm slammed across my chest, halting me abruptly.

"Check out that tree," he ordered.

The tree in question had a twisting main stem and drooping foliage. Its gray-brown bark was chiseled roughly and housed clusters of thorns in nasty-appearing hooked pairs. Quite large, standing at least ten meters tall, the tree drooped forward, its leaves hanging down in a manner similar to the South's famous weeping willow trees. I wondered perhaps if the tree possessed some sort of edible berries and sought to inch closer, but Peter's iron arm kept me back.

"There, Mandy, among the branches. Do you not see it?"

I peered again, but for the life of me, glimpsed nothing. What on earth was he getting at?

"Where…?" I questioned.

"*There.*"

I followed the direction of his finger and suddenly noticed a green, leafy twig with… bright black eyes? I backed away from the protection of his arm.

"Oh jeez!"

"Isn't she a fine boomslang?"

*It* dangled in the shade of the thorny tree, its blunt head endowed with large emerald eyes that never blinked as it swayed back and forth, looking for prey. *It* was my least favorite thing in the world: a snake.

"If I'd walked under that tree, I could have run right into her!"

"She probably would have moved away. Boomslangs are quite shy and prefer to hunt chameleons and small birds."

"Is it poisonous?" I asked breathlessly.

"Oh, very. A farmer who was bitten in the village next to our farm died within two days. The venom causes massive internal bleeding. Still, a beautiful, beautiful snake, hey?"

"Yeah, a real dandy."

"Would you like to get a little closer, lass, to take a better peek?"

"No," I declined, striving to appear confident but uninterested. "Perhaps another time?"

Peter rolled his dark eyes and I knew full well he recognized my abhorrence of snakes. Ever since Eve, hadn't our sex loathed the vile species?

"You're hot and fatigued. Let's take a break and drink before moving again."

So, nearer the evil emerald snake than I would have preferred, I chugged down some water, immediately feeling better. Our break was too short. Peter forced us on with a relentless determination.

The grass had become nearly waist-high and I concentrated chiefly on watching my step. Peter's safari hat was drenched with sweat and constantly slipped down over my eyes. Less than five minutes into our hike, I exclaimed, "Oooh... what's that horrible smell?"

Peter paused abruptly, his spear-like walking stick held ready. "Over there," he cautioned.

In the dense shade of a pod mahogany, ghastly-faced vultures hopped over the mostly-devoured corpse of a large antelope.

"It was a kudu," whispered Peter.

The twisted horns of a large male gleamed an unnatural crimson in this late morning light. Two species of vultures vied for the remaining flesh clinging to the large buck's bones. Four or so large, brown birds with disgusting red heads curved like striking snakes assaulted the corpse. The other five or so buzzards were smaller, with white heads stained pink. Tearing and plucking savagely, they attacked each other in their frenzy, their curved beaks perfect for grabbing the decaying flesh from the bones as well as warding off any competition.

Peter studied the area. "There," he whispered, pointing. I was barely able to make out the single footprint, but instinctively knew it belonged to a cat.

"Lion?" I gulped.

"No," he disagreed after a moment's study. "A leopard. This was the doing of one cat—lions generally hunt in prides. It's strange she didn't drag her dinner into that large sycamore fig.

Either something scared her off or, more likely, the kudu proved just too big for her, its oversized horns handicapping her ability to drag it into the tree."

I'd read that leopards drag their kill into tall trees, not only to protect them against scavengers like the vultures, but to leisurely feed upon the rank corpse over the following days.

"Do you think she's still around?" I whispered.

"No," Peter said reassuringly. "Leopards are mostly nocturnal and it's evident that she's finished here and has left the vultures to clean up. You have nothing to fear."

I noticed, however, that he gripped his combination walking stick and spear more tightly. Cautiously, Peter skirted the area, I following him much too closely.

We marched through the warming morning until noon, luckily seeing nothing more dangerous than birds, before I slowed down, hot and thirsty. My legs strangely ached and itched, and I desperately needed to go to the bathroom.

I cleared my throat. "I need to use the bathroom again."

"Go ahead while I keep watch." Peter grinned and swept his arm toward the bush, indicating that the whole world was my toilet. The area we traversed was fairly flat, the scrub mopane thrusting up through the dry grass. There, beyond a small log, a clump of bushes provided a bit of concealment, so I wandered as nonchalantly toward the mound as possible. I made quick work of it and had just finished when I noticed my legs and gasped aloud.

"Everything okay, Mandy?" boomed Peter's voice through the bushes. Peter had discreetly turned around, his sweat-stained shirt visible from where I crouched.

"I… um… " I answered, flustered. "I'm not sure. There seems to be something strange on my legs."

Peter turned around slowly. I straightened, pulling up my briefs but leaving my jeans just below my knees to hobble away from my outdoor urinal.

"What is it?" he asked matter-of-factly, nary a muscle moving in his tanned face.

"My legs, they're… they're bruised or something." It was the 'or something' that alerted him.

"Let me check."

I was caught between modesty and confusion, but his almost doctor-like manner reassured me, so I waddled toward him. Peter studied the dark, swollen bruises and numerous welts on my upper legs and couldn't disguise his swift intake of breath.

"Are there any more?" he asked.

"I don't know," I admitted and reluctantly dropped my pants down to my trainers. Upon my calves and ankles rose masses of bruised areas. Peter ran a finger over one of them and shook his head grimly.

"Feel those swollen bumps? I'm afraid you're infested with ticks, Mandy. We'll have to remove them."

"Ticks? You mean like dogs have, or that giraffe we saw today?" My voice sounded shrill even to me.

Peter thrust his spear into the dirt. "Unfortunately, lass, just like outdoor pets get. You have at least twenty here upon your legs and perhaps even more on your arms and torso. The ticks perch upon the long grass, waiting for an opportunity to transfer onto any passing host. You're their latest victim."

I don't know if many Americans have ever had the immense pleasure of finding their body riddled with tick bites. These small oval bloodsuckers burrow themselves under your skin and drink as gustily as vampires, swelling up to three times their original size. The only way to remove them is by either pouring rubbing alcohol onto your skin or lighting a match near the entry hole so that the tick backs up, disturbed by the heat. Unfortunately, we had no rubbing alcohol, so Peter removed the few remaining matches from my pack along with the old kerchief I'd swaddled my hand in after the lion attack.

"Try to hold steady, lass. If you jerk, I might burn you."

I'm certain I made quite an elegant picture standing there with my trousers wadded about my ankles while Peter gently placed burning tips of matches against my skin. Immediately, the first brown tick emerged, bloated twice its normal size with my crimson blood. Peter smashed the bug and used the cloth handkerchief to mop up the tiny droplets of blood oozing from my bites. For fifteen minutes he probed, burned, and squashed the parasites. Most, fortunately, were restricted to my ankles and lower legs, but one had burrowed near my crotch and I hastily turned away my flushed face as Peter's deadly matches annihilated the tiny beast. The Zimbabwean then asked me to lift my shirt. Fortunately, he spotted only one, an inch or so above my belly button.

"They prefer low-lying grass, so most end up on your legs. You seem clean, lass," he announced finally. "Hand me your water bottle." He splashed all my remaining water and most of his over the oozing wounds to clean them. "That should do for now," Peter said casually, as I hastily pulled up my pants, my face burning.

"Your trousers are much too loose on the bottom, allowing ticks to burrow in. See my trousers, Mandy, how they're stuffed inside my boots. I have an idea."

Peter untied both of his boots and using his knife, cut off two long but equal lengths from his laces.

"Use these," he said, "to bind the bottoms of your pant legs."

The wounds inadequately cleansed, I wrapped the laces tightly around my pant legs.

"We need to wash your wounds better," Peter announced. "You must know that it is possible to get a disease called tick-bite fever. If, in a couple weeks, you have a terrible headache, chills and fever, and feel the need to vomit, we'll check with your doctor and indicate you had a tick infestation. They'll prescribe you medication to ward off the symptoms." I loved how he had used the word "we."

On this happy note we started off again, my thirst increasing as my tick bites throbbed. Blood seeped through the cloth, making small circular spots upon the filthy denim to mark the tick wounds. The bites itched painfully and soon another misery arrived to torment me as small flies, attracted by the oozing blood, swarmed about my stained jeans.

Peter discovered another animal trail, which made traversing the rough terrain a great deal easier. We trudged in near silence for two more hours that hot midday, my thirst reaching monumental proportions and my discomfort knowing no bounds. Upon the beaten-down trail, I observed many small piles of pellet-like droppings which were bigger than the impala's he had pointed out before, but less shiny. By now, I was rendered too tired and uncomfortable to ask Peter anything about what might have produced them.

We finally reached a dry riverbed and Peter hesitated for a moment before heading toward the edge of the sandy wash, where the dirt seemed several shades darker. I could see now the huge footprints in the wash, obviously made by elephants. He leaned down and, poking his walking stick into a footprint, dug furiously. After a few moments he squatted and touched the soil. "There's water here," he announced.

I didn't say anything, but moved closer, licking my parched lips. "Where? I don't see any."

"The elephant knows that in dry season water is far away, so she digs with her heavy feet and trunk into the edge of what looks to be a dry riverbed like this. If she's lucky, the water will seep to the surface."

Peter began scooping out the soft sand like an intent badger. I bent over, intrigued in spite of myself. Lo and behold, after burrowing out a pit of six or so inches, water seeped to the surface. Brown and filthy, it was, nevertheless, wet. I was so thirsty I wanted to throw myself on the ground and lower my lips to the muddy fluid.

"Easy, lass," Peter laughed. He continued digging into many more adjacent footprints and as the water continued to rise, he scouted about, searching for dry needle grass to place atop the murky water.

"Wait a few minutes. The water will clear above the straw and you can drink."

We waited five before Peter bade me to lie down and scoop up enough of the liquid to slake my thirst. A true gentleman, he allowed me the first taste before leaning down and drinking himself.

"It's not good enough quality," he announced after slurping noisily for a few moments, "to clean your tick bites. We'll have to find running water to do that."

"How far away from a river are we?" I asked.

"Too far. If we headed north, we could run into the Luvuvhu, but there are no rivers in this area. There's one a great deal further south called the Nkulumbeni, but it would be unwise to venture in that direction. The road is too far off, and the region is famous for its lions. No, we have to travel this way to find the

Limpopo. It's the safest and easiest. There's some more moisture in that footprint. Take one last drink. Who knows when we will find water again."

# *Chapter 20*

*Water bottles empty and thirst barely slaked,* we embarked on our hot march again, pausing only once within the next two hours to rest under the shade of two twin thorn trees, which Peter announced were really false thorns. My throat and mouth, again parched from lack of water, could barely produce enough saliva to wet my lips. Peter caressed my hand before gently pulling me to my feet to return to our killer pace.

I'd read that midday and afternoon are the hours you see animals least on game drives. We were fortunate it held true for us. Only startled pink doves, a few circling birds of prey, and distant snorting that Peter said were rooting warthogs, disturbed the dry, hot afternoon.

The sun had perched directly overhead when Peter suddenly gave a cry of triumph and lunged forward. I have no idea from whence the small stream of flowing water originated, only knowing it was welcome beyond belief. A few moss-covered boulders sidled up against the low embankments and from them, in the shape of a widening fan of perhaps thirty yards, grass obstinately grew green in the dry heat. A few pale-brown birds scattered at our approach as Peter quickly knelt near the base of the rock.

"Do you see," he pointed, "how it seeps from the stone? There must be some sort of underground stream."

He knelt and drank, and then moved aside for me. I lay prone in the cushy green grass and gulped noisily. And, because the water was so plentiful, I even dared wash my face. Peter then gathered his dirty second-hand sports bottle and my own two-liter bottle, and filled them to the brim.

"We'll rest here awhile," he said, "and drink more. I'd like to scout around, but since water is very scarce in this region, many dangerous animals may come here to drink. I think it would be a good idea if you accompanied me."

It sounded like an excellent plan. I took one more drink and then noticed the comical expression on his face.

"What?" I asked expectantly.

"It's just, Mandy, that the water has made interesting designs upon your face…"

The small pool of clear water allowed me to catch my reflection. The dirt made a boundary of filth on my streaked face. Dust outlined my eyes and I resembled some kind of scary African Halloween mask. I giggled and dunked my face completely in the water. The refreshing shock was welcome as I scrubbed my face briskly with my hands.

I leaned my still-dripping face upward and asked, "Is that better?"

"Much, lass. You're passably kissable," and he followed the words with the deed. "Let's rest a bit and wash off your tick bites." I obeyed and used my rinsed-out water bottle to splash and cleanse the sores.

While I was busy, Peter scanned the depths of the bush. A strange, high, jolting laugh came from not far off.

"*Bere!*" exclaimed Peter as he gripped his spear.

"Bere?" I repeated.

"The hyena. They laugh before they kill."

From Peter's expression, I gathered that a hyena was something I wouldn't want to run into personally on foot. I remembered their nerdish appearance when I'd viewed them the first time from the safety of my car.

"I saw a couple the other day. They're dangerous?" I asked nonchalantly.

"Very. The brown less so, because he is more solitary, but the spotted run in packs."

He humped his shoulders to mimic them. "They're so fierce they will fight the lion for its kill. Did you know that the brown hyena drinks no water? The blood and fluid from the carcasses gives him enough. The female has a false penis and is a ruthless and skilled hunter."

I gulped. "A false penis? Jeez. Are the brown found in this area?"

"Not as much as the spotted."

The sound repeated itself and intensified to a mixture of high-pitched screams, strange gurgling squeals, and definite dog-like whines. Finally a distant answer floated back, followed by another message before all fell silent.

"It must be a brown. The spotted can live in clans of up to eighty in number, but that sounded like only two speaking. The spotted's shouts are different, more like *whooo-oop* and rising in strength at the end. Sometimes they even seem to giggle. That is why they're referred to as the laughing hyena. They're more a predator than the brown, and thus much more dangerous. I believe I should scout around."

I nodded, though I didn't want him to go. Peter rose abruptly and balancing his walking stick-spear on his shoulder, disappeared into the bush. Within ten minutes he returned, dragging something large and white behind him.

"I saw no hyena," Peter announced, "but look what I found." The joy of a little boy parading his newly-found treasure sparkled in his face as he adjusted an immense skull with huge, hollow eyeholes before me.

"Is that an elephant?" I asked incredulously.

"It is indeed. I believe this one died in its forties of disease."

"Now how could you possibly know that?" I asked.

He laughed. "Remember how I told you about the teeth?"

Peter worked and wiggled at the jawbone of the massive skull, finally managing to dislodge a couple resistant bicuspids.

"Do you see here? This is his fourth row of teeth. As I told you, elephants are born with six rows only, and each row lasts him about ten years. The elephant must eat up to fourteen hours a day and consume perhaps a hundred and seventy kilos of grass and leaves to maintain his massive weight."

I did a quick mental calculation. "Let's see, if a kilo is a little over two pounds, that means roughly three hundred and forty pounds or more a day. Amazing," I exclaimed.

"It is indeed, lass. As herbivores, they must feed continually. Fortunately, they're not picky eaters. They'll eat anything and everything that is chewable, including sticks. They grind and wear down a row of teeth every ten years or so, mostly from the rough bark they chew."

"But you say this elephant was in his forties?"

"Yes. Let me prove how I know." He dug around with his knife and in the light of the flickering flames, pointed to twin embedded rear sets of teeth.

"Two rows left. He must have been injured or sick. The sick here die quickly, as the lion and hyena take out the feeble first."

In his hand rested a small block of elephant teeth.

"May I have that?" I asked suddenly.

Peter seemed surprised. "You want the elephant teeth? But, of course."

"I'll keep it as a souvenir of how I was lost in the bush with you."

Peter smiled and settled on the ground, using the skull as a backrest. "Tell me more about your family, Mandy." One would have thought it was a pleasant Sunday afternoon over tea on the terrace. "You have other family than your mother?"

"Yes. I'm an only child, but Ken, my cousin, was raised by my folks. My father died a couple years ago, but my mother and cousin still live in Florida. We reside in Orlando, though actually Mom's on the perimeter of the city. She's still quite mobile and can get around. She took me to the airport."

"Your cousin, is he older or younger?"

"Older. He is trained as a scientist and owns a computer company. He's quite successful."

"You don't care for him." It was a statement.

"How'd you work that one out?"

"There is no warmth in your voice when you speak of him."

I hesitated. A daytime sliver of moon showed itself just above the thorn trees.

"My cousin is difficult, but only a little more so than my mother," I said lamely. "Ken is very conservative and has an opinion about everything. He doesn't really like women or people of color that much. He believes he's… naturally superior. It doesn't matter that I have a college education and support myself; I will never be his equal, not in his eyes or my mother's. He's clearly the favorite, even though he's not Mom's son."

"I understand. The living blood of a family can make one's shoulders stoop."

The simple statement for some reason warmed me. "How true. I suspect my cousin feels superior to everyone because of his education, intelligence, and upbringing. He *is* brilliant after all."

"And his brilliance blinds him to life? He's not married?"

"No, and I think he never shall."

"And you don't like him and feel guilty because of it?"

"Yes, and because he always finds fault with me, thus making it difficult for me to love him."

"In the village near where I was raised in Zimbabwe, there was a wise old man who told many stories similar to the one about the mosquito."

I smiled at the memory of the delightful tale.

"He died not fifteen years ago," Peter continued, "in a most horrible way." He paused and sighed. "The old man originally came from Lesotho. He was short and crooked and age had twisted his fingers so he could barely hold a cup. Most of the Shona from my region were tall. The men from Lesotho are small, perhaps because of the harsh conditions of their mountainous country."

I had to interrupt. "I'm afraid I don't know where Lesotho is."

Peter didn't seem surprised. "It is a small, high country totally surrounded by South Africa. It is said that Old Man Lightning strikes there more than any other place in the world. Anyway, some people disliked the fact that Sipho had come to that village, married one of the chief's daughters, and was revered as a wise man. He was not one of the "locals," you see, though he had lived in that village since before I was born. Most accepted him, but not a man named Loben. Loben was like your cousin. Anyone not like him was unwelcome. He hated whites, the Ndebele, and any Shona who disagreed with him. He beat his wife and said it was because Tira was stupid and slow. And then, even as she was pregnant with his fifth child, he cast her out and married a girl of sixteen from the neighboring village, saying Tira dishonored him by only bearing daughters.

The tribal elder sent Loben to speak with Sipho in hopes that the old man would give his son some advice that might straighten him out. Loben did as instructed and spent over an hour at the old man's hut. Afterwards, he disappeared for three days. Sipho did not appear the next morning and finally his granddaughter, very concerned, went to check on him. There she found him with his head smashed in, the brains oozing out and the ants… the ants had been at his body and had started to clean the flesh from his bones. It was a scene most horrifying, my father said."

I shuddered at his unique manner of speaking.

"Worse yet, it was determined that he had died just around the time Loben visited him. When Loben finally returned home from his wanderings, he was arrested by the police. But he had an alibi. He had left Sipho in good condition, he said. The old man must have slipped and fallen, hitting his head against the hearth stones. It was true that there was blood on the bricks."

"You think he was guilty?"

"None of us will ever know. After Sipho's death, Loben said that God had come to him in a vision during his days in the bush, and ordered that all outsiders must be either driven away or killed. If not, God would smite them down, just like Sipho. Soon, there were attacks upon the nearest white tobacco farm, and one of our neighbor's daughters was killed by cattle stampeded by the intruders. Loben was clearly the leader, stating the whites had robbed, raped, and stolen from his people and didn't deserve to live in Zimbabwe anymore. Anyone who disagreed with him was branded a traitor, and Loben suggested that all who weren't "true Zimbabweans" should leave. My family knew it was just a matter of time, so we sold out and moved to Zambia. Later, I started university in South Africa to study the care and maintenance of game parks. I've never gone home. To this day, Zimbabwe is full of voices just like Loben's."

"I'm sorry," I said and squeezed his hand, saddened his handsome face had turned so bleak.

"You rested now?"

"Enough. Lead the way, sir."

# *Chapter 21*

---

*We both felt fairly strong and adopted a brisk pace* through the scrub forest. Only twice did we spot game. Once, while crossing the sandstone hills and mopane treed plains, I glimpsed a small herd of impala, the dominant male lifting his head inquiringly before allowing his herd of does to continue browsing. The second buck species, as we headed gradually southwest, was angling down toward the Mazanje waterhole, and bounded parallel to us for a full minute before crashing into the bush. Its large, veined ears, white underbelly, and short spike-like horns were unfamiliar.

"The steenbok," announced Peter as if reading my mind. "They're generally active only in the morning and evening, and are very territorial. The interesting thing about this species is it buries its urine and feces. Pretty thing, hey?"

"Yes, very."

We walked for nearly an hour. More observant now, I asked Peter readily about various plants, insects, and birds. I noted not only dove feathers, but speckled white-and-black ones which Peter identified as the Guinea fowl. When a *kek-kek* sound emitted from a thorny tree, I glimpsed a small white-and-black bird exhibiting boundless energy.

"It's the white-winged tern; it's found throughout this region."

And everywhere, anywhere, swarmed the endlessly busy ants. From small black troopers to enormous brown warriors, they scurried under our feet, up tree trunks, or clung to swaying spears of grass. Wasps and dragonflies flitted about and a butterfly, shot through with white and scarlet, alighted upon early blue flowers. Once Peter stopped to point out a lone suricate that barked out a swift warning as we neared.

"That's the sentinel. The mammals are quite social and many are around, but they're in hiding." Peter suddenly halted, turning around to smile at me from where we stood on the low crest of a sandstone hill. The trees seemed greener here and huge pod mahoganies grew thickly.

"We are not much more than two hours or so from the waterhole. We'll be home soon, Mandy, for many tourists drive there to watch the animals drink."

A thrill of excitement coursed through my veins; my return to civilization was only a couple hours away! We were carefully ascending the rather steep incline when a strange sound followed by a trumpeting roar and the heavy crash of brush filled the air. High-pitched screams eerily surrounded us. Peter tensed, his sandy head jerking back and forth as he tried to determine the origin of the sound.

"What is it?" I screeched, my hand grabbing the dirty sleeve of his khaki shirt.

"It sounds like a woman and..." He took off at a dead run.

I had no choice but to follow, my slippery trainers a poor substitute for his boots in this rough terrain.

We plunged down the rest of the incline before jerking up short at the most horrible sight I've ever seen. The prostrate woman was already dead, but for some reason the elephant didn't seem to believe that fact and continued trampling her limp form. I leaped forward to help, but Peter grabbed my arm, jerking me back.

"There's nothing we can do. She got between the matriarch and her baby. It's the elephant's revenge."

The pachyderm finally turned, lowering its long trunk to touch the woman roughly. The bloody woman didn't move so finally, her blood lust satisfied, the agitated elephant backed off. The matriarch paused, fanning her ears and roaring. A small herd of elephants emerged from the trees. Four stood full-grown, but three were babies. The murderess lifted her trunk and bellowed again, and this time the elephants shuffled off. The smallest, standing not much higher than four feet, seemed reluctant to leave and the impatient matriarch batted him on the rear with her trunk, forcing him to obediently move along. We waited for what seemed an eternity until only the faint sound of their steady retreat and the clicking noises of insects filled the air.

"We can go down now," whispered Peter and I followed him to where the prostrate victim, covered in sand and blood, lay motionless. My heart lurched, for it had not been just a lone woman. Strapped to her back, under a soiled red blanket, lay the humped form of a baby. Only the blanket was not naturally red— it had originally been colored a light beige and blue. I turned my head away in agony.

"This is sad. Sad indeed," grieved Peter. We drooped there in the churned-up sand and gazed helplessly at the lifeless pair.

"Who is she?" I asked, barely able to keep back my tears.

"In this area, many refugees from Mozambique cross. It is likely her husband preceded her to South Africa and sent a message for her to join him."

"But why was she here alone; alone with her baby?"

"I don't know," said Peter heavily. "But one thing is for certain: if we leave her, the vultures and hyenas will arrive in a matter of minutes."

He was not far wrong. Already, dark specks in the brilliant blue dome of the sky circled and dipped ever lower.

"What shall we do?" I asked. I now cried silently. What a cruel, horrible fate!

Peter dropped to his knees and turned the woman over. Her body may have been brutalized and broken, but amazingly enough, her smooth, brown face remained unscathed. She appeared no older than sixteen. Peter untied the blanket knotted just above her breast and gingerly lifted out the baby. I suspected it was a little boy, not more than six months old, but it was so bloody and smashed it was difficult to discern its features.

"Help me dig a grave," Peter ordered. "While only a short-term solution, it will allow us time to get away from here before the dangerous scavengers arrive."

Peter chose a shady spot under one of the mahogany trees and we both knelt and dug with our hands in the soft sand. It did not take long for the two of us to scoop out a narrow trough wide enough to roll the bodies into. The Zimbabwean arranged the still corpse of the young girl with the baby held in her arms. Though bloody, they both appeared asleep.

"We need logs and rocks to place on top so the animals can't dig them up so quickly," Peter said. "Could you go try and find some?"

A decent-sized log lay not twenty feet away and I hurried over to it. As I tugged and pulled, I harbored a strange feeling that if I just kept busy, the horror of what had happened to the young girl and her baby would somehow disappear. A soft tenor voice lifted in song, forcing me to glance up from my sweat-popping task. Having scraped sand over the bodies of the woman and her baby, Peter now stood, his arms held stiffly to his sides, and softly serenaded the pair in a language I did not understand. The beautiful dedication to her and the nameless baby enveloped me in sadness. I don't know if he sang to God or to the powers of nature, but profound grief resonated from his reverent voice.

I whispered a silent, hurried prayer as well, one filled with questions and accusations. Why had this young woman, scarcely out of girlhood, died so horribly? Why are some allowed to live while others have their fragile lives literally torn from them?

The gentle serenade ceased and Peter strode forward to help me drag the heavy log over the makeshift grave.

"*Zorora nerunyararo,*"[2] he uttered huskily.

In less than fifteen minutes, a dozen logs and stones lay stacked upon the girl's and her infant's still bodies.

"We didn't even know her name," I mourned sadly as I fruitlessly rubbed my dirty hands upon my streaked jeans.

"Would you feel better if you knew?" asked Peter. Telltale trails made narrow paths through the dirt lining his tired and filthy face.

"Somehow I think so. Yes. I would have liked to know their names."

"Then name them," he ordered softly.

---

[2] Rest in peace in the *Shona* language

The chatter of what sounded like magpies and the buzzing of persistent insects were the only noises as I pondered what to call this nameless woman and her poor, dead child. Finally I said, "I will call her Esther, and for the child, a name I've discovered many workers in South Africa have: Precious."

Peter flashed a pained smile. "Then their names shall be Esther and Precious. Hurry, Mandy. As you can see, it is not safe to walk the wild ways. We must get to the waterhole before dusk."

Numbly I marched away from the burial site, mind whirling as I tried to make sense of it all. Who, besides us, would ever know that this ragged woman, so desperate to join her husband and family that she risked death, lay buried under log and rock? Would anyone besides the grimly silent Peter and me ever know she'd been trampled to death by an irate elephant? Where was the justice of it all? What had made her approach that dry riverbed at precisely at that instant, forcing her to come between the elephant and its calf?

I have always been a staunch believer that a benevolent God watches over us and when something bad happens, the Lord enables something good to come from it. As my tired feet tramped through the dust, I could not fathom any good resulting from that poor woman's death.

Perhaps if I embraced a religion such as Hinduism I'd have felt more settled. If one believes in reincarnation, there must be some satisfaction that when this life ends, you simply begin another. Christians aren't so fortunate, believing you're only given one shot and when your allotted time is up you proceed either to heaven or hell. But that tiny baby—what happened to him? Had he already sinned so much he deserved to die? I'd read somewhere about how souls are recycled. Had baby Precious already arrived back at the soul factory, ready to be inserted into another body that would hopefully have a better run of it next time?

I fretted inside as I trudged through the bush behind Peter and swatted at the blue dragonflies attracted to my sweaty face. God has a plan—He must have! And if He had a grand design, what was his plan for Esther and baby Precious? What benefit had their little lives brought? Worse yet, what was *my* purpose? I battled myself the whole rest of that horrible march until Peter finally took pity upon me.

"Stop," he ordered abruptly. He crouched, his arms resting upon his legs, staring at the ground.

I lifted myself from my misery, my damp eyes finally focusing on what he examined. The spoors were fresh and clear, only slightly smeared by the damp soil. We had come across a seep hole where algae-scummed water, dotted by small tufts of grass, made a shallow muddy place where swallows whirled above and plovers shrieked warning. The imprint Peter examined reminded me of a flower with five blunt petals, the topmost being broadest. The six sets of tracks abruptly ended at the perimeter of the seep hole.

"Can you figure out what this track is, ma'am?" Peter asked, peering up at me. I crouched beside him, grateful for the rest. Our sorrow had propelled us at a killer pace.

"A lion?" I suggested. To me, any large track must belong to that merciless killer.

"Not even close, my lady," he returned, grinning.

Peter grabbed a dry stick and poked at the half-dry mud. "The lion's paw has a flat rear knuckle-like area with four toes at the top." He drew it carefully in the gooey earth.

"This is an important track to recognize since it can mean the difference between life and death. Another dangerous one is this."

He traced two curved beans roughly one-and-a-half inches long, facing each other.

"I know that one!" I said excitedly. "It's the Cape buffalo."

"Very good, Mandy. They rarely travel alone, as we've noted. And this dainty little one is the impala. But this spoor is deep and reveals the animal's massive weight. You see, the track is quite broad and indicates that heavy legs must support its incredible size."

"What is it?" I breathed.

"From the size of the track, it can only be the white rhino. It is similar to the hippo in many ways."

He drew a spoor resembling the rhino's, only with more elongated toes.

"Both, you see, have broad, flat tracks. These animals lumber; they cannot prance or spring since their weight is much too heavy for that."

"Is… is it alone?" I managed.

"I don't know. The white rhino is often found in small familial groups. They're interesting because they defecate in what are called rhino middens. I glimpsed one back there near the gulley, but I believe you didn't notice it at the time."

Peter was absolutely correct; I'd been incapable of noticing anything that morning. My eyes flitted about as I probed the dense foliage, remembering the butchered rhino near where I'd run across Peter again.

"If it's a rhino, mightn't there be poachers about?"

"Perhaps, though the rhinos this deep into Kruger Park are more protected since military presence is so pronounced."

"Are rhinos ever dangerous?" I asked, wishing I could wipe his troubled frown away.

"The white, not very, but the black is unpredictable and solitary. Since I suspect these are white's tracks I'm not so leery. He'd probably just ignore us. Look here—see the little beetle with the long antennae?"

A black-and-red beetle scurried across the print, oblivious to our presence.

"He's amazingly quick."

"Yes. It's a longhorn beetle, named such for his antennae, which natives thought resembled miniature horns. He's harmless enough."

I lifted my water bottle and took only one deep gulp. He smiled, noting my conservation.

"Are you alright now?" he asked. It was the first time he'd made any reference to the death of the young woman and her child.

"No," I replied, gazing straight into his russet eyes. "I will never be the same after witnessing that."

"Some things are not meant to be forgotten. Let's rest, since we've been pushing so hard. Why don't you sit on that log while I find us something to eat."

I sank down on the dirty tree trunk near the seeping water, and my tired eyes drifted back to the spoor. Certain I could identify a rhino in the future, I scanned the dense woodland for wildlife. A dull yellow bird with a black head hopped in to drink from the algae-laden water before flitting off. Red dragonflies hovered over the smelly water, searching for who knows what, and a sad dove moaned in a nearby tree.

Peter returned only a few minutes later and handed me some round, hard nuts.

"Crack the outer shell," he instructed. "You'll have to smash it against a rock."

I did, revealing tiny brown seeds, which upon consumption tasted bitter and oily. I didn't even bother to ask him what they were; our Spartan meal simply fell into the gastric generalization of *food equals survival*. We munched silently for several minutes, Peter scanning the turquoise sky and tangled woodland, while I rested and choked down the unappetizing nuts.

"It is a sad thing about the woman," he finally said.

"Yes," I answered simply.

"But, strangely, I believe her time must have come."

Suddenly my cousin's arrogant face flashed before me.

"That's a bunch of hogwash!" I said hotly, the fermenting thoughts of the morning welling to the surface. "It was NOT her time. I refuse to believe we have a specific time to die. We have accidents or make mistakes for sure and… and we are subject to folly and sometimes major missteps… but… but… I can't believe, I refuse to believe, that was all the time she was allotted on earth."

Peter said calmly. "The elephant did not mean to kill her, Mandy. The matriarch was simply protecting her own."

"And that's it? So Esther and Precious, at the moment of their births, were destined to die in that wash. It could just as easily have been us!"

"It wasn't our time," Peter stated calmly, cracking another nut against the flat surface of the rock near where we sat.

"Nonsense! No one has a specific time. I admit I'd like to say that if she truly was an evil woman she got her just desserts, but the baby… the baby! That woman only wanted a better life for her child and a trampling by a hairless mammoth was her reward?"

"We *all* want a better life. Some of us just have to strive harder to get it."

"Because someone's black?"

"Maybe, or perhaps belongs to the wrong tribe, practices the wrong religion, or simply suffers from the fatal mistake of being born in the wrong place or wrong time. If I'd been born just three hundred kilometers across the border in South Africa, my life would have been so different. My parents wouldn't have lost their farm, and maybe I wouldn't have become a nature guide. If I'd been born a Shona and poor, it could have been me crossing this treacherous park seeking to find a better life, not her. I don't understand why we are born to certain circumstances, I only know we have a duty to utilize what we have and strive to live in harmony with nature."

"My cousin says we all have a purpose as well. He says some of us count and some of us don't."

"Ah, that sounds like the novel *The Fountainhead* by Ayn Rand."

"You've read it?" I couldn't keep the disbelief out of my voice.

"Of course, it was in my father's library."

It seemed strange to be sitting in the middle of the bush, discussing a novel about New York in the 1920s whose protagonist, Howard Roark, believed in the philosophy called objectivism.

"Did you... you *like* the novel?" I asked, holding my breath for his answer. I hadn't liked it much myself.

"I don't know. It is interesting—the belief that the achievement of one's own happiness is the total moral purpose of life. That is the ruling philosophy of the book, isn't it? I think that it must have been written by a white South African during apartheid."

I wanted to laugh, but couldn't. The truth was too pathetic. "It's an interesting philosophy and I would have to agree that while we all strive to be happy, it's much more important to take the chance of bettering ourselves to rise above our station. I don't believe there's just a massive populace that can be thrown aside by the elite few, trampled to death like that woman."

"You and your cousin fought," Peter said wisely. He seemed proud of the fact. "He sought to be your oppressor."

"My oppressor? Yes. But in hindsight I can see we didn't fight nearly enough. As a young woman, I let my cousin spout philosophies, usually narrow and cruel, without as much as a whisper of defiance. I either lacked the courage or maintained the foolish notion that if I remained quiet, his stinging words wouldn't really matter. So I always let Ken speak and never contradicted him. I realize now that was a sin. If one doesn't speak out, you're agreeing with whatever the speaker states."

"You are becoming a radical," said Peter mildly. "You would be put in prison in Zimbabwe. My father said that God is the rainbow. Wherever the arch landed, the rays hit the ground and the fragments shattered, scattering different colors and different ideas into every land. I'm not sure I believe in God, but I do believe in rainbows."

"I believe in rainbows too," I said and we joined hands.

"And your cousin, he is a first-class asshole?" He said the last word just like Arnold Schwarzenegger and I had to laugh.

"Ken is *challenged* in many ways. He lives a little life."

"So tell me American Miss—what do *you* believe is the most important thing for a man to do?"

"Any *person* should strive to take care of those they love, learn something new every day, and bring about something good in this world during their life." My own answer stunned me. Until this very moment I wouldn't have uttered any of it, not truly believing it. The miracle was that I did believe it.

Peter smiled, his teeth flashing brightly in his darkly tanned face.

"That is much better than the ideas from *The Fountainhead*, or those of the cousin whom you despise. But for now, my lady, we must make it to the waterhole. You're not tired anymore?"

"No," I said and took the uplifted hand he offered. It was not far now.

# Chapter 22

---

*The only game we spotted on that final trek to the* waterhole was another giraffe. Old, its reticulated spots peeked dark and grimy from under a layer of dust. Its tongue proved brilliant for the task of reaching around thorns to pluck at the succulent leaves. We watched him for over five minutes as he munched contentedly upon the long, slender leaves of the peculiarly twisted thorn tree.

"You could learn a lot from the giraffe," said Peter, who had broken off his examination of the tall mammal to stare at my neck.

His brilliant brown eyes locked on my throat disturbed me. "What on earth do you mean by that?"

"The giraffe, for all his neck, has no vocal chords. He is mute—the silent one of the bush." The corner of his mouth twitched and puckered.

It took a moment for his subtle insult to sink in.

"Why, you…"

I bent and picked up the closest object I could find to fling at my tormentor. A bone, gnawed and dry, whistled through the clear air. He gracefully dodged the clumsy toss and we laughed together like children.

The waterhole we were making for was not an actual waterhole per se. It consisted of a large, concrete reservoir that fed water into long, narrow troughs so the animals could drink. Forty minutes later, as we rested at the top of a small knoll, Peter pointed to the man-made structure.

"Do you see it?" he questioned. I did indeed. In the distance, a small metal windmill revolved slowly in the slight breeze. Just beyond that, the faint glint of circular white concrete indicated we had nearly made it to Mazanje. "The river is just there."

I peered in the opposite direction where the water gleamed, a white, fast-moving blur.

"Why did they build it here when the river is so close?"

"The banks in this region are very steep and cliff-like above the quite narrow shores of the river for nearly three kilometers. The middle of the Limpopo is strewn with boulders, generating white rapids. A small waterfall, less than a kilometer upstream, feeds this section, and it runs much deeper and swifter than further downstream where the river widens out. The lesser creatures found it difficult to access water safely, as did the rangers, so this waterhole was constructed in the early nineties."

I studied him. Peter appeared confident but wary with his broad shoulders and homemade spear held ready.

I brushed my hair away from my face. It had long since broken free of its elastic tie.

"May I borrow your little notebook?" Peter asked. I obliged immediately and using my airline pen, he began to write. "The number belongs to my sister Elizabeth, in the Cape. If... if for some reason we get separated, call her."

"We won't get separated," I stated confidently and studied my wonderful man as he replaced the notebook carefully back inside my pack.

"I noticed you recorded the hijackers' license plate number."

"I did indeed. Heads are gonna roll!"

He laughed and extended his hand. "It's fairly steep here, Mandy, watch your step."

That last little trek to the waterhole was uneventful. We must have not been much more than 100 meters away when Peter straightened.

"Did you hear that?" he hissed. I stopped, nestling close to him.

"What is it?" I whispered.

"I thought I heard a motor," Peter said.

"We must be nearing the waterhole. Maybe it's a car!" My voice rang jubilantly. Peter hesitated, cocking his head to listen.

"Perhaps it was not a motor at all," I said, disappointed when only the chatter of waxbills hopping about black-thorned acacias answered my cry.

"More likely it was just the wind turning the wheel of the windmill to pump the water," returned Peter.

"That's probably what it was," I disappointedly agreed.

"We're very close now, lass." He joined one of the countless animal-made trails leading to the waterhole and I followed. The dry, short grass brushed our pant legs as we walked briskly toward the windmill. This particular path was quite narrow, probably formed by countless impala, nyala, or bushbuck heading toward the reviving water.

The brush made brisk whisking sounds as we hurried through it. My eagerness and haste made me careless. I longed to sing out in happiness; I was finally returning to civilization! It would just be a matter of minutes before Peter and I would run into a car and be whisked back into the safety and cleanliness of

Shingwedzi camp. The license plate numbers and descriptions of the hijackers hurried my steps even more as the desire for revenge crowded its way through the joy.

The trail made an abrupt curve. We could not have been more than 25 meters away from the windmill when a horrible stench assailed my nose. Just to the right of us the ravaged remains of a huge male kudu littered the beaten-down grass. The poor beast had not been felled by an animal, but had died from a gunshot right between the eyes. Its hindquarters had been carefully and meticulously cut away. The poachers had not desired its lovely curved horns or majestic head to mount upon their wall; their need had been simple—food. It did not take long in this midday sun for scavengers to catch a whiff of the decaying flesh. I glimpsed a black-backed jackal in the distance, slinking through the tall grass, and high above, lappet-faced vultures circled, ready to swoop down upon the decaying meat.

It was then that I heard what Peter had earlier; the grind of a truck's motor pulsing through the midday heat. A large, open truck full of armed men roared into the clearing where the poacher's lifeless victim lay.

"Oh, no!" I hissed, clinging to the false hope that perhaps they hadn't seen us. How guilty we must have looked, standing not twenty feet from the butchered buck. Peter grabbed my arm and pulled me backwards.

"Stop!" cried the lead soldier, who wielded a deadly-looking rifle. Peter thrust me behind him.

"*Eish!* Run, Mandy! Make for the river! These are not our friends!"

We tore through the brush, the thorns grabbing at my wrapped ankles. I could hear the rapids below, and the shrill screech of a fish eagle. But far louder was the roaring, reckless pursuit of an armored jeep and shouting soldiers. The way was rugged, and the jagged rocks and brush aided us for a while, but our pursuers were determined.

The steep cliff served as an insurmountable barrier and we both halted abruptly, clouds of dust and debris surrounding us. Peter shoved me behind him and raised his makeshift spear.

"Get behind me Mandy! Don't shoot! We are lost! I have an American woman with me. Don't…"

Those were the last words Peter emitted. I remember it now in horrifying clarity, the long seconds ticking brutally in demented slow-motion. Like harpies, the camouflaged soldiers descended upon us, jumping from their truck and swinging automatic rifles up to their shoulders.

I'm not exactly sure, as I tumbled to the ground behind Peter, what it was the handsome Zimbabwean intended to do. I think that perhaps he'd just meant to ward them off. Or, was it simply the hunter and tracker's instinct in him that compelled him to raise his rudely-made spear at them, or were his hands held up in truce? As the shots rang out I know I screamed, the hysterical pitch of my voice filling the late-afternoon air.

Several bullets hit him simultaneously and Peter tumbled backwards, plummeting over the cliff. The soldiers lurched forward, aiming their rifles at me, ready to fire. I heard the frightful splash as his body hit the water, and crawled in the dirt like a lizard to peer over the crumbling cliff. Peter rocked face down, his body swirling in a slow-motioned circle; the crimson of his blood tingeing the water. The current caught him and tossed him to and fro. Then he was tumbling, twisting over and over in the frothing white water to be pummeled and forced downstream.

The half-dozen or so troopers circled me, their rifles held ready as I screamed in helpless confusion. A soldier pulled me roughly to my feet. Helplessly sagging in agony, I gazed at the silent murderers who stood so mutely at the edge of the cliff overlooking the charging river.

The finality of death should be a simple concept, particularly when one is stranded deep inside a huge game reserve where living creatures struggle every day for their lives. Of course I understood that. Hadn't I witnessed my grandparents' gentle transition into death and watched my father battle tooth and nail for every feeble breath during his last few weeks of life? And of course, there had been the helpless young woman this morning, trampled to an early demise by the belligerent elephant. But this was different. How can something as vital as a living man—as energetic as the vibrant Peter—finally succumb to death? The reaper, now perched in the massive fig tree bordering the watering hole, grinned as the river carried away his prize, his scythe signaling to the circling vultures that yet another tidbit awaited them amongst the rocks when the river finally calmed.

"He's not a poacher!" I screamed finally, and the camouflaged soldier who had helped me up found it difficult to keep hold of me. It finally took two more of the stone-faced men to restrain me, as I fought and writhed in my helplessness, held firmly by the trio.

"He is not a poacher," I cried hysterically. "You're murderers, murderers! Peter! Hurry! Take your vehicle and find him! He might still be alive!"

The soldiers shifted, suddenly made acutely uncomfortable by my loud incriminations. What they had viewed as a rescue rendered them only abuse. Their leader edged closer; a thin, wiry man with short, kinky hair dotted abundantly with gray. His dusty sunglasses rebuffed my hysterical face. I continued to scream as he solemnly removed them, his broad nose flaring widely under eyes so dark they were rendered opaque. He studied my frantic form in silence. I shrieked again and would have sought to batter him if I had not been held so firmly by the three soldiers.

"He was not a poacher!" I repeated; my voice high and tight.

The officer didn't even flinch at my piercing cry. "Yes, he was," the commander said quietly, responding to me like a parent does an inconsolable child.

"He wasn't. Peter was just taking me to the waterhole because we'd been hijacked and lost. He was my guide and friend."

"He is Zimbabwean?" my tormentor asked matter-of-factly. "His name Voorhurst?"

"He *is* a Zimbabwean, but his name is *Peter Leigh*, not Voorhurst!"

"You have his papers?" asked the unfazed leader. "I thought not. He," said the officer, peering straight at me, "is a notorious poacher. Hijacking women tourists, stealing our precious game. You are safe now." He gestured towards the distant waterhole where the brutalized kudu's left hind leg pointed toward the sky, locked grotesquely in rigor mortis.

"No, no," I moaned.

"It is no great loss," the troop's leader continued, "that another of these invaders has perished. It is one less problem for me to deal with. One less problem in a sea of problems."

I protested weakly. "Peter is an innocent guide who helped me. I was lost... lost in the bush, and Peter came to my aid."

The tall man snorted. "Innocent, him? Of course not. He came illegally into our country as a poacher. He knew the consequences if he was discovered."

For some reason, I couldn't control my body's massive shaking. The head soldier's voice gentled as he pondered me.

"It is only important that you are safe, ma'am. You *are* the missing Miss Phillips, aren't you? That Zimbabwean, he kidnapped you?"

Hadn't this bastard heard anything I'd said? I didn't respond because my voice had dried up. I could only shake my heavy head. Speaking was wickedness and silence only slightly less so.

He continued, taking my lack of response for agreement. "We have been searching days for you. Your jeep was found abandoned across the Limpopo. The tires were shredded from the rough road and the hijackers ripped out the console and DVD player and removed the seats and much of the engine. You are fortunate to come out unhurt from such uncouth men." He spat towards the cliff. "His kind has no regard for life."

I could only stare blankly at him as the now idle soldiers milled around, oblivious to Peter's plunge into the river. One appeared to be chewing gum.

"I have forgotten my manners. My name is Sergeant Thabo Magandi. It is time for us to take you to safety."

I must have suddenly sagged because the troopers' iron grip loosened. They now struggled to hold me up rather than restrain me.

"Do not worry about this poacher. We will take care of his body… if the crocodiles leave us anything to find. He was nothing, nothing at all and cannot harm you anymore."

Peter, nothing? The man who had saved me, taught me, filled me with hope, and most importantly, loved me. Guilt and fury overwhelmed me.

I violently shrugged off my captors, who respectfully stepped back. I had no knowledge of how wild and tough I appeared to them. My chestnut hair resembled greasy, matted dreadlocks and my normally pale skin was burned beyond recognition and stained with charcoal. My bug-ridden clothes were torn and filthy and my trainers had two gaping holes in the toes. I swayed, but refused the men's offered help. Staggering feebly toward the cliff's edge, again I searched the rushing river. Nothing. No Peter, no hope. I whirled on the sergeant.

"I've told you before; he was not a poacher. You've committed a crime against an innocent man and I'm going to turn you in to the proper authorities!"

Sergeant Magandi appeared puzzled. "Your *so-called* friend raised his spear at us. Innocent men do not attack the military."

"He was only trying to protect me," I whimpered.

My rescuer's face softened. "I think I understand. It is a woman's nature to grieve for even the most callous of men, even a *tsotsi*."

"I'm begging you. Send the jeep downstream. His name is Peter Leigh. Check with Kruger Park's headquarters. He'll be on their roster as one of their tourist guides. Please."

Thabo Magandi hesitated before barking out something to his men. One of them eased his rigid stance and stooped to retrieve my pack, which he respectfully gave me.

What causes the sprite Mercy to elevate her bedraggled head during such tragedy? I have no knowledge from where this phenomenon springs and why some men live their entire lives without a shred of it, while others suddenly exhibit it out of the blue. Thabo was one such man. His eyes gentled as he studied my wild, disheveled form, and took pity upon me.

"It is clear," he announced to his half-dozen troops, "that this man is important to Miss Phillips. Radio Private Lwazi and have B Unit search downstream."

When no one moved, he turned abruptly and shouted in a rapid tribal tongue. The youngest of the group peered unblinkingly at him.

"Yebo,"[3] he said finally, and shouldered his rifle. Two of the men stalked over to examine the butchered kudu, while the others sidled up to their vehicle, their backs to me, to begin barking into a walkie-talkie.

In a nearby tree, a beautiful gray lourie with dark, haunting eyes, who now I could identify because of Peters's tutelage, called out *heey-heey*. Peters's voice, its memory still rich in timbre, echoed in my ears. *The grey lourie is evil. She rested upon our roof the day my father's farm was overrun and called "Go away, go away."*

And now there she perched, whining nasally "*waaaay, kay-waaaay*," over and over again. The translation was simple: Wake up stupid woman, you are asleep. Go away—*kay-waaay* from Africa—you bring bad luck! Wake up and face the reality of Africa and the rest of the world: some people matter and others don't.

The lourie mocked my dismal state for another full five minutes as I crouched in the dirt and chaos reigned about me. Resigned and still disbelieving, I finally rose and gathered up my tattered knapsack before heading to the waiting truck. Later, in the rear of the vehicle, as it roared and bumped along the rocky road belching black smoke into the purity of the African bush, I wept.

---

[3] A widely used term among many Southern African tribes, signifying agreement.

# Chapter 23

*For all those who state that South Africans are inefficient,*
heartless, and hopelessly mired in endless bureaucracy, I must
confirm that, at least in this instance, they are all wrong. I was
treated, after those traumatic events, with only the utmost civility
and kindness. A helicopter carried me to Louis Trichardt, a city
not far from the Punda Maria gate, and deposited me in the local
hospital. There, I was endlessly prodded and poked until finally
being pronounced fairly fit. I suffered from a mild case of head
lice, bug bites, and numerous ticks that had escaped Peter's
scrutiny, as well as countless bruises and scratches. Numb, I was
wheeled into a semi-private hospital room for overnight
observation. I took a long, hot shower and was presented a
nutritious meal. The American Embassy in Pretoria, after being
notified of my mishap, promised to send out a representative the
very next day.

My wallet, passport, and camera were missing from the
remains of the trashed jeep, and I could not leave the country
without some form of identification and cash. A middle-aged
Afrikaner man, the florid-faced representative of Kruger Park,

.ı Shingwedzi and my room was emptied. It

ıd Peter's bag, clothing, ID, and park badge.

, promised a full-blown search for Peter's body

ıd with clean clothes and my plane ticket, the

had thankfully left in a drawer by the bed. The rest

.gings would follow. Frankly, as his portly figure

ıd through the swinging door, I could not even

er exactly what those other belongings were. I wanted

g from Peter's and my room. My heart had morphed into

. was surprised the doctor could even find a heartbeat.

Once the sympathetic Kruger representative had departed, a ,ustling African nurse fussed and cooed over me, her delightfully rounded countenance exuding a maternal and soothing sense of order as she tucked me in just like my mother used to and begged me to try and sleep after my "dreadful ordeal."

"You call me or another Sister if you need anything, Mama. Try to sleep."

The lights of the pale room dimmed, the room door swished, and only the faint scurry of busy hospital staff passing occasionally outside the small window of my swinging door indicated the hospital still functioned. All abandoned me to supposedly sleep and get better. Instead I lay rigid, my fists clenched as the vision of Peter's bullet-ridden body sailing over the cliff, and Thabo's hollow explanation regarding his death, crowded out any possibility of sleep.

It was that final, horrible realization that I'd been able to do nothing to save my innocent, cherished Zimbabwean that finally overwhelmed me. I remembered my earlier thoughts—had it only been just that morning after we'd witnessed the trampled refugees' bodies in the wash?—regarding people's destinies. Couldn't we have taken another path or found a tourist road? For hours I rehashed every memory and every step that had led my beloved Peter to the anti-poaching troops. Why had God or fate intervened, snuffing out Peter's life and leaving me here alone, to tremble cowardly under the thin hospital sheet as I recognized I had been the real culprit in his demise?

The kindly nurse had placed the battered backpack and my meager personal belongings, fetched by Mr. Pretorius, inside the small cabinet beside my hospital bed. I leaned over and removed the small notebook where I had recorded all my sightings in Kruger. The last entry, in Peter's bold hand, denoted his sister's first name and Capetown number. I couldn't bring myself to call her just yet. It would needlessly worry her. Surely, surely, they would find him.

I tossed most of the night, only drifting into a restless drowse at 4:00 a.m. It was a night far more hideous and lonely than any spent lost in the bush.

The American Embassy chastised me royally. Somebody from up north flew me down to Pretoria the following afternoon and unfortunately, it was now my deserved punishment to sit restlessly in front of an overweight man sporting a hideous orange-and–purple-speckled tie who supposedly represented the United States of America.

"I think," Mr. Dobbs said, "that you have been rather foolhardy to travel alone in South Africa as a single young woman."

His second chin with its unceasing wobble distracted me from his fatherly words. I tried to focus.

"I wasn't aware," I said quietly, "of a travel advisory issued for single young women visiting Africa."

He scowled. "No, though *any* reputable travel agent would have suggested that you join a tour instead of traveling unescorted."

"I was not *unescorted*. I was traveling with one of Southern Africa's best rangers."

"Yes. It was indeed fortuitous that Mr. Leigh located you after that violent hijacking. But to rent a jeep by yourself, unaccompanied… what could your travel agent have been thinking? There are all sorts of wonderful cruises, tours, *Club Meds* in Mauritius to be had. It was simply foolhardy! You're lucky to be alive. Thank God I'm here to sort all this mess out. It's regrettable about the deceased. The military here are more inclined to shoot first and ask questions later. You'll be happy to know, however, that there'll be no complications with the South African government regarding your involvement to worry about."

Thoroughly chastised, I fidgeted as my bloated compatriot wrote furiously, his government-issued pen flying over the bureaucratically long paper. Form UTW (only used for unaccompanied truant women) proved a monumental task, and he bit his lip. Mr. Dobb's balding head, starched white shirt, and pained expression made him a perfect candidate for a poignant remake of an outdated fifties sitcom. His stance and slightly vacant expression indicated how annoying the embassy employee really thought my dilemma was.

"When will I receive my duplicate passport?" I asked.

Mr. Dobbs clucked sympathetically under his tongue.

"You know, after 9/11 we have had to send all our passports to the National Passport Center back in the States to be reissued. Of course we will place an *Urgent* tag on yours, but it will still take some time."

"And Peter... Mr. Leigh... has his... his body been recovered?"

"I'm sorry, Ms. Phillips. There's been no word. As far as I know, SAPS is still searching for his remains."

A thin Asian man had taken some hideous passport photos immediately after I'd filled out all the new forms, and whisked everything away without fanfare.

"And how will you be paying for this?" Mr. Dobbs asked, his pen poised as he leaned forward, double chin wobbling.

"My wallet, passport, camera, and jeep have been stolen. Consequently I have no money. How would *you* suggest I pay?"

He didn't like my retort and his pale blue eyes narrowed. "You don't remember your Visa card number and expiration date?"

"Ah... not off the top of my head."

Mr. Dobbs seemed clearly affronted. I guess all travelers to South Africa are supposed to memorize the 800-number to their Visa card company in case they get hijacked. I'd put that on my to-do list right after I touched down on US soil again.

"I'll arrange for the embassy to advance you some emergency cash then. René in accounts will help you with your Visa card. I'm afraid you'll have to remain in Pretoria until your duplicate passport is available and your plane ticket can be changed."

"How long will that take?" I asked.

"A week, ten days, who knows? Call us every day and we'll update you on the progress. Have a good day." I was dismissed. Stiffly I rose and pushed back my chair.

You've got to love bureaucracy! When all else fails, it continues to survive, just like the cockroach. However, I must admit that by the end of the day I did have some money, a place to stay, and the promise from a bored René that my Visa card would be DHL'd within the next couple days. I hid in my dark hotel room while I recuperated, grieved and checked the unblinking room phone for messages every ten minutes. I watched reruns of *Oprah* on satellite TV while sipping orange juice and eating scones. I couldn't stomach anything else. After two shows, I have to admit that Oprah did more to revive in me the fact that I was an American than anything else.

My sorrow didn't diminish. I'd read about the five stages of grief, but seemed stuck somewhere between anguish and denial. The next day I phoned Peter's sister, no longer able to put off the inevitable, but only got a tinny recording of a cheerful voice indicating she was away on business and would get back to the caller. I never heard from her, though I phoned several times each day. On the fifth day, I resolutely spelled out my home address and phone number in Florida, praying Elizabeth would eventually call.

My passport arrived six days after filling out the application. Clearly a world record! My ticket changed and reissued, I soon sat numbly in business class, contemplating first how to deal with my family and second, how to continue life without Peter. My worries were entirely founded as I spent the next several days striving in vain to explain my experiences and perceptions to those around me. The numbness of my mundane routine, even with a new job, proved the most comforting thing to me, since I received nothing but criticism from my family during those first dark days after my return. When the announcement arrived less than one week after my return that Josh intended to marry his teenaged girlfriend, I wasn't even fazed.

My friends and family simply shook their more knowledgeable heads, comfortable in the assumption that something like *this* could never happen to them, since they weren't foolhardy sorts like me. My cousin proved particularly irksome. In his nasal tones, he insinuated that while I had been close to losing my marbles before embarking upon my adventures, now, after the hijacking and death of Peter, I had clearly lost them. I ignored him—remaining silent through his nonstop lectures. Ken found my mute gaze intolerable, desiring me to either agree with him or at least counter, so he could put me down.

"You're different," he accused after dropping by that second Saturday afternoon after I'd returned. Ken and my mother had taken to *popping in* to check on what I later overheard my mother term "the mental invalid."

"Is that bad or good?" I asked indifferently. "Since you couldn't stand me before, what's the big deal?"

"Couldn't stand you? What ridiculous nonsense. You're my cousin and I love you. Somebody has to. But I have to admit you're a goddamned mess, Mandy. While the death of your Zimbabwean friend was "unfortunate," you're probably better off. Long-distance relationships never work."

"Whatever."

"That's your only response—whatever?"

"Yup. You didn't know Peter, so don't you dare comment on him. He was my soul mate and my beloved, and because of my stupidity, I've lost him, and consequently, any hope at future happiness."

My cousin hesitated. "No word from his sister or the South African authorities?"

"No," I swallowed, barely able to hold back my tears. "Nor the police, who promised to phone me if they discovered anything. I think… I believe his body was never recovered. The Limpopo River is full of crocodiles."

Ken barged ahead. "You didn't know the last name of his sister?"

"Not her married name. Peter never relayed the name of her new husband, either. We didn't talk that much about his family. "

Ken toyed with a coaster before reaching into his pocket to remove a gold-embossed card. "You know, I have this friend I attended undergraduate school with. Jeff moved back to Orlando just six months ago. Maybe he could give you a call."

It took a moment for the identity of his friend to sink in. "Jeff, the defense lawyer?" I really hadn't expected that my nerdy cousin would try to match me up. I waved the proffered card away. "I'm not interested right now. Please. Could you close the door on your way out?"

A peculiar expression flitted over my cousin's face. His tone actually sounded contrite. "I'm truly sorry about all that happened, Mandy. You know, Josh was a swine to cheat on you. Hey, I'll phone in a couple days, okay?"

Frankly, I wouldn't care if he ever phoned.


Mom stopped by the following weekend as I scanned an article about the upcoming elections in Zimbabwe.

"Why do you keep reading that boring stuff?" she asked, dropping her handbag onto my new chintz couch. I'd sold the adulterous other one.

"Just want to keep informed," I answered mildly as she followed me into the kitchen. Since she was here, I might as well cook a meal. My mother rambled on about the brilliance of a new TV series she was watching, her fantastic bridge club, and the retired and *very* interesting single brain surgeon who'd moved down the block from her.

As I cut my roast chicken into bite-sized pieces, she shocked me.

"I have a present for you, Amanda. Actually, it's from both Ken and me."

"A present? It's not my birthday."

"I, um. Well, you know Jeff, Ken's friend?"

Not again. I steeled myself. "The lawyer?"

Mom wiped her mouth daintily with her napkin. "Actually, Jeff isn't a lawyer anymore. He's a private investigator and Ken and I hired him to find Peter's sister."

Stunned, I dropped my fork.

"Anyway, Jeff managed to locate her. Something about a fire in her tour office and a new number—but to make a long story short, this Elizabeth wants to meet you."

I stammered. "M...meet me?"

"Yes. She wishes to meet the woman her brother loved. So here..."

Mom slid a thin envelope across the cherry table. I recognized the emblem from Azure Travel.

"Ms. Raymond, the agent from your tour agency, was key to finding his sister. And... once we had... it seemed only natural to obtain you an air ticket. You must visit her to gain some closure."

"My new job... " I sputtered.

"Damn your job, Mandy! You've suffered an ordeal. I can't imagine my baby girl lost in the African bush. How brave, brave you were. And then, on top of it, to lose the man you'd grown so fond of. A man... who was likely your peer."

I forced myself to close my mouth. Her admission seemed inconceivable. Someone more suited to me than Josh?

"I haven't been a very sympathetic mother," she continued unsteadily, "and... well, Ken and I need to do better by you. And... about that job. Certainly, a woman of your qualifications can easily find another position if they refuse to grant you this needed time off." She folded her hands primly upon the table.

Stunned, I opened the plastic travel envelope. Nested inside was a round-trip ticket to Durban, South Africa.

"Durban? But Elizabeth lives in Cape Town."

"Apparently her aunt lives in Durban, and Elizabeth finds it more convenient to meet you there. Something about its proximity to Kruger? I guess she's been dealing with the authorities regarding Peter."

I turned the ticket over in my trembling hands. "It's for a week stay?"

"It's refundable and changeable. I had no idea how long you would need so... we... we paid more for the ticket so you could change it if necessary. You leave Tuesday. Is Durban a *safe* city, Mandy?"

Her question bewildered me. "I guess. It's a large city on the Indian ocean, miles from Kruger."

She cleared her throat nosily, took a deep breath and said the bravest thing I'd ever heard from her. "If you'd like, I'll go with you." Mom's roast chicken sat idle in its thick gravy, her green beans losing some of their bright color.

I smiled shakily. This was a side of my mother I'd never encountered before. She *hated* air travel. I leaned over to kiss her slightly wrinkled cheek. "I love you too, Mom. Thanks for this. But, I...I'm fine traveling alone. And you're right. I do need closure. This is the nicest thing you've ever done for me."

My mother actually appeared startled. I rose and trotted to the oven, pulling on my oven mitts to remove the apple crumble we'd made together. After helping with the dishes, Mother gingerly hugged me before leaving for the safety of her condo.

"Amanda?"

"Yes, Mom?"

"Well, it might be awhile before I see you again so stay safe. Promise to call me before you leave?"

"Will do. And Mom…tell Ken thanks for me."

# Epilogue

*While late winter in South Africa, it was still quite hot in* Durban. I arrived on a Wednesday evening, the humidity pouring through the newly opened doors of the Boeing jet. I removed my sweater, which had valiantly fought against the chill of the cabin, and gazed upon the turquoise Indian Ocean sparkling in the distance. I collected my bags and dragged the same maroon suitcase that had survived my first trip through customs. A small, willowy woman with silver hair and a dentured smile held up a hand-written placard. It read: *Welcome Miss Phillips.*

I pulled up in front of her and smiled. "You must be Mrs. Giles, Elizabeth's aunt."

"In the flesh," she said, her British-South African accent, so much like Peter's, falling gently upon my tired ears. "Welcome to Durban, dear."

She drove a small pickup truck like a pro and chatted about the weather, the diminishing influx of tourists that always marked the long winter season that, strangely, fell over our traditional summer holiday, and how her garden was progressing most famously, though she really needed extra help. I felt like I already knew her.

"How is Elizabeth?"

"Chuffed you're here. Elizabeth couldn't change her meeting with the estate agents today. Hopefully, she'll be done quickly, as she's so eager to greet you and fill you in on everything we learned about Peter's tragic encounter with the SAPS."

Estate agents? Oh God! I hoped Mrs. Giles and Elizabeth didn't feel they owed me anything of Peter's. I couldn't bear it!

Mrs. Giles pulled up before a quaint antique and furniture shop whose spotlessly clean windows allowed the discerning shopper a wonderful glimpse of the goods inside. She pushed open a glass-paned door equipped with an old-fashioned tinkling bell and held it wide for me as I dragged my case through. A young blonde lady greatly resembling Mrs. Giles rushed forward, her hands outstretched to enfold mine.

"I'm Elizabeth," she introduced herself. "Lisa's niece and Peter's sister. How wonderful for you to come. Aunt Lisa has a flat in the back where you'll be staying. You can freshen up there and then we'll chat."

The shop was quite spacious and, due to its fairly close proximity to the tourist beach, maintained a moderate business in winter and an excellent one the rest of the year. Items from the Voortrekker[4] days, as well as antiques that had traveled from England and Holland to South Africa via various immigrants, dotted the shop. While pricey, the items were well-chosen, obviously meant for a discerning clientele.

---

[4] Dutch pioneers who came from the Cape to settle in the lowveld during the 19th century.

"Come along," said Mrs. Giles, "but be careful of all the knick-knacks. My lands, this store is way too much work. But that will be remedied soon."

I cautiously rolled my large suitcase through the narrow passageway between all the tables and crockery, and followed her through a door at the rear of the store. I smiled in delight at the sight meeting my weary eyes. The landing led into a lovely courtyard draped with bougainvilleas and dotted with miniature orange trees planted in huge, sand-colored pots. A trellis leaned against the two-story wall, covered in white and pink roses. A wrought-iron table, complete with a huge green canvas umbrella for shade, sat next to a small dripping fountain overlooking wooden flower boxes stuffed with petunias, marigolds, and daisies.

"We have a back garden as well, but it's so pleasant to take our breaks here when the shop is open."

A door made of stained glass and dark wood opened into the foyer of the house. The entire home, decorated from generations past, whispered of quality and an enduring reverence for the past. Mrs. Giles lived her trade and over the years had carefully collected antique pieces to adorn her lovely abode. Elizabeth watched me with anxious eyes of an identical brown to her brother's as her aunt led me to the back apartment.

"Here's your room. You must be knackered after your long flight, so rest as long as you need. We'll be waiting for you in the shop when you're ready to chat."

The large, sunny guest bedroom faced the Indian Ocean. Complete with canopied bed, an antique dressing table, and quaint tea stand, it overlooked the sea and the terraced garden. Someone had placed a vase of Shasta daisies upon the table and a profusion of tiny pink carnations hung outside the windows in rectangular window pots.

I marveled at the view as I unpacked my bag and hung up my clothes. Standing at the wide windows, I observed the tropical garden. A unique feather-duster tree stood near a sweet gum, and the long and narrow yard was spotted with queen palms. Mrs. Giles obviously loved her flowers. A scarlet clarodendron sparkled in the bright light while trumpet creepers, whose orange-red flowers trailed over the wooden fence, vied with brilliant honeysuckle. It made for a dazzling canvas planted with care. Several Yesterday-Today-and-Tomorrow flowers bloomed in tri-colored harmony while sending out a heavenly scent. I realized I had tarried long enough; it was time. I turned just as a tap sounded on my turquoise-painted door.

"It's open."

The door swung wide and a form leaning on a cane appeared, only a shadow before the glaring brilliance of the sun without.

It couldn't be! The apparition moved deeper inside the quaint apartment and there he stood, one arm in a sling, a fresh scar running from his chin to his cheekbone, and a full black walking cast encasing his right leg.

"Peter!"

"Yes, lass . . ."

I flung myself at him. "Gently," he warned fruitlessly as I encased him inside my loving arms. Wincing a bit, he energetically returned my tearful kisses.

A long while later, Peter lowered himself gingerly into the overstuffed cream easy chair positioned under the bright chintz curtains fluttering in the partially-open window. I sat at his feet on the wooden plank floor and leaned my dizzy head against his uninjured leg. "I thought you were dead!?"

"So did I. But I guess the Fates had different plans. I must admit to losing my appetite for white-rafting after being thrashed about for so long in the Limpopo."

"But you were shot—I saw the blood!"

He tsk-tsked. "They were actually only lackluster shooters, those soldiers. I took three misguided bullets and this graze on my face, but wouldn't you think they'd be better shots than that?"

The fact he could joke about it, that his warm, living flesh had survived, brought me to tears again.

"Your leg?" I stammered, wiping my eyes.

"A compound fracture. The bullet hit a stubborn bone and exited through my thigh. I may need another surgery—but except for a sexy limp, I'll be fine." He lifted his slinged arm slightly. This bullet luckily missed my elbow and a third bullet bounced off my ribs. This graze on my face was the worst I'm afraid; I nearly bled to death."

"*Now* you really look the part of a rough-and-tough game park ranger." I caressed his leg. "Who found you?"

"Now, that's the *real* tale. An illegal named Themba Mikosi, who was traveling with his wife and two children, ran upon me on the Mozambique side of the river, as I barely hung onto a partly submerged log. He and his family remained with me for nearly a week until I could travel. Themba says, quite modestly, that he jumped into crocodile-infested waters, dodged two maternal hippos, and nearly drowned inside a whirlpool to save me. I owe him my life. He placed his family in great peril to stay with me. I must say I have never eaten better crocodile tail stew than his wife, Sibu, cooked. You will have to try it sometime."

I digested what he said as we basked in the late afternoon sun, my nose crinkling at the heavenly scent of gardenias.

"Why did no one contact me?" I finally managed.

Peter placed rough fingers in my hair and massaged my scalp. "Remember that poacher, Ian Voorhurst... the one I was mistaken for?"

"Yes."

"Themba knew the location of his base poaching camp on the Mozambique side of the Limpopo River. After Themba and Sibu managed to ferry me to a SAPS post across the river, we 'negotiated' with the army."

"I'm afraid I don't understand."

"Themba sought to immigrate to South Africa. So, with some assistance from me—added by acute embarrassment on the part of the local SAPS after what their misguided anti-poaching squad had done—we traded his information for a South African residence permit. The "sting" was quite hush-hush for a while. After I contacted my sister, she informed me that a private investigator hired by your mother and cousin had communicated with her. I requested they not reveal anything until I could speak to you in person."

"My mother agreed to that? She knew?"

"I told you that your old mum and I would get along."

I smiled through grateful tears. "And Themba?"

"God bless my sister and aunt. The only way we could legally acquire my rescuers' immigrant status was if they were sponsored. So, Themba will help Aunt Lisa with the antique shop—doing the heavy lifting, deliveries, and whatnot—and Sibu will cook and clean and raise her two rambunctious boys."

"Your aunt mentioned Elizabeth was at the estate agents when she picked me up. I thought… I thought they were discussing your will."

He laughed. "Estate agents are realtors here in South Africa, Mandy, not barristers. She was just securing a fine little cottage down the block for Themba and his family." Mutely, I rubbed my face against the worn denim of his good leg.

"And what's this, lass?" Peter said lightly and leaned over to finger the elephant teeth he'd given me weeks ago, which now hung on a silver necklace around my neck.

"The only tangible thing I had to remember you by."

"Well, I'm sure I can find a sight better piece of jewelry than that to have you remember me by, love."

We both smiled gently as the sun perched above the ocean, dangling like some ripe orange ready to pluck. I reached out my hand to seize the exhilaration it embodied. I was no longer lost in the bush, forlorn and uncertain. I had not a second to waste with my beloved before my own elephant arrived.

The End


**\*\*If you enjoyed this book please check out other Books by Loren Lockner on Kindle or in Paperback \*\***

**Timberline Trail-**Romantic Suspense located in the wilds of Southern Alaska.

**Love Never Dies-**Ghostly Romantic Suspense located in Santa Barbara, California.

**Under a Desert Sky-**Romantic Detective Mystery located in Palm Springs, California.


## **\*\*Loren Lockner also writes Mysteries, Fantasies, and Picture Books under the name Tyan Wyss\*\***

**Bouncer** (Detective Mystery)

**Return to Mt. Snagra** (Epic Fantasy)

**Ghostwriter** (Ghostly Mystery)

**The Solitaire Prince** (Romantic Fantasy/Fairytale)

**Coming Soon: The Keeper of the Keys** (Fantasy) & **See Saw** (Detective Mystery and sequel to **Bouncer)**

*Heart of Africa*

Loren Lockner

# Heart of Africa

Loren Lockner

Printed in Great Britain
by Amazon

35961923R10135